ten of the best

School Stories with a Difference!

WENDY COOLING is a highly respected and well-known children's book consultant and reviewer. She taught English in Inner London comprehensives for many years before becoming head of the Children's Book Foundation (now Young Book Trust) where she initiated the Bookstart project, now being implemented nationwide. She is a regular guest on radio and television programmes and is the compiler of several anthologies, including *Centuries of Stories* and *Mirrors*, both published by Collins.

ten of the best

School Stories with a Difference!

Edited by
Wendy Cooling

An imprint of HarperCollinsPublishers

Also edited by Wendy Cooling
Centuries of Stories
Mirrors

First published in Great Britain by Collins in 2002
Collins is an imprint of HarperCollins*Publishers* Ltd
77-85 Fulham Palace Road, Hammersmith, London W6 8JB

The HarperCollins website address is www.harpercollins.co.uk

3 5 7 9 8 6 4

ISBN 0 00 713339 1

The editor asserts the moral right to be
identified as the editor of the work.

Printed and bound in England by
Clays Ltd, St Ives plc

CONTENTS

Margaret Mahy
School Days

All the fleas ran up your back

MARGARET MAHY has been a nurse, a librarian and is New Zealand's best-known children's author. She became the first writer outside the United Kingdom to win the Carnegie Medal, for *The Haunting*, winning the same award two years later for *The Changeover*. Her other novels include *Memory*, *Twenty-four Hours*, *Riddle of the Frozen Phantom* and her soon-to-be-published *Alchemy*. In 1993 she was awarded New Zealand's highest honour, the Order of New Zealand, which is only ever held by twenty living people at any one time.

Margaret Mahy

School Days

There are two worlds, aren't there? Look through the window and you immediately see the everyday world of families, of pets, gardens, lawns and gates. Roads and footpaths run past those everyday gates tying family homes to parks and shops and schools. That is one world.

But there is that other world, too – the world of magic and amazement that swallows us when we read a story. As a child I wanted to drag stories off their pages and into the everyday world around me. And I didn't just want to live in the story. I wanted to *become* the story – to be the story's hero. Being the hero worked quite well as long as I was playing in the yard at home. But somehow it never quite worked once I went to school, though sometimes it almost did. And everyone knows there are two school lives – the classroom life and the playground life, both very different from one another.

I began school during the war when even little children were expected to lead an orderly classroom life – a life that was quiet and stern. Out in the playground life was just as noisy and wild as it is today, though back then boys and girls were not allowed to play together. Over in their part of the playground boys invented adventurous games – war games – racing around, holding out their arms on either side, making aeroplane noises and pretending to shoot each other down. In the girls' part of the playground we made houses for ourselves in between the lower branches of the trees that ran along one edge of the playground. I played there with the rest of the girls, but I was always a little jealous of the boys. Their games looked so exciting. Over and over again I found myself longing to bring adventure into life around me – longing to become the magical hero of a fantasy – and suddenly, out of the blue, school offered me the chance to invent a story that was all my own. All the same, things did not turn out the way I thought they would. My story surprised me more than it surprised anyone else.

I didn't plan my story. It began accidentally because there was going to be a fancy-dress ball at my school.

'A fancy-dress ball!' said my mother. 'What do you want to be?'

'I want to be a fairy,' I cried, imagining myself as beautiful as early morning, flying on delicate pearly wings, a dress of pink foam trailing behind me. Waving a starry wand, I would amaze everyone with my spells.

'Oh, a lot of people will go as fairies,' my mother said. 'Why don't you go as a witch?' She turned to my father. 'In a way, she has the face for it,' she said. It was almost as if she thought I would not be able to hear her.

A witch! My own mother, who loved me, thought I looked like a witch. I knew that I had a long face with a big chin, but I had never imagined that I might look like a *witch*. And yet, after all, witches were even more wild and magical than fairies. Witches were *dangerous*, so being a witch at the school fancy-dress ball might be a bit of an adventure. I suddenly felt I might have a lot of fun being a witch.

My father made me a pointed hat out of cardboard, rolling it, gluing it, and then painting it black. While I practised swishing a broomstick and cackling, my mother made me a black dress. I thought I was rather good at cackling, and perhaps I was. I certainly cackled as if I meant it. (I still do!)

The great night came. All the school children turned out, ready to sing and dance and to surprise each other. And my mother was right. There were lots and lots of fairies, but only one wicked witch. Me! I showed off, skidding around on the slippery floor of the local hall, waving my broomstick and cackling loudly. The fairies slid away from me. Even the cowboys and Indians looked nervous. We danced the dances we had been taught to dance at school, we ate a small supper of scones and pikelets, and then the fancy-dress ball was over. The pink fairies became ordinary little girls once more. The cowboys and Indians disappeared. The cackling witch disappeared too – well, *almost* disappeared.

The next day at school a few children called me, 'Witchie!' They didn't really mean any harm. It was just ordinary teasing, and if I had been really clever I would have laughed and taken no notice. After all, anyone could see that I was just another one of the school children. Yet somehow or other the name-calling made the cackling witch spring to life in me once more. After all, if I kept on being a witch those two worlds – the everyday world and the storybook one – might melt into one another.

'Yes,' I told those other children, 'I *am* a witch. I can do magic spells, and I also have a poisonous bite like a snake.'

But my story just did not work in the school world. Other children caught up with me on my way home from school shouting, 'Witch! Witch! Witch!' at me. Some of them just wanted to tease me, but there were one or two of them who were actually angry with me, and one girl swung me round yelling, 'Witch!' into my very face. I grabbed her arm and bit her just to prove to everyone how poisonous my bite could be. How I longed to turn those shouting children into frogs! They would have respected me then. I would have been surrounded by hopping frogs, all croaking and pleading and promising that if only I turned them back into children, they would be my friends forever. The strange thing was that I wanted other children to *like* me.

Anyhow, I certainly did not enjoy being a witch without magic, particularly when I was on my way home from school. Sometimes, I would run as I left the playground, making for home with other children chasing after me. Sometimes, I would turn in at strange gateways and hide on the verandas of houses that belonged to people I did not know. I would knock on doors, telling the astonished women who answered my knocking that other children were chasing me. The women would look down at me, puzzled and frowning, for they were busy, and of course they didn't know just what was going on outside their gates. In any case, there was nothing they could do to save me. In the end I always had to go back to the street and keep running towards home. That story – the story of the witch with the poisonous bite – had certainly not worked out the way I had hoped it would. No one respected me because of it.

All the same I learned something from all this – something which altered the way I felt about the adventures other people were having at school. And to this very day, more than fifty-five years later, I can still feel that lesson working in me.

There were small shed-like shelters in our playground into which we were expected to cram ourselves if it began to rain while we were outside at playtime, and during one particular break I joined a group of children to torment another girl. I have no idea to this day why we ganged up on her, and do not even remember her name. I only know that we drove her into one of the shelter-sheds, pointed at her and cried out a nonsense rhyme that I still remember:

Stare! Stare! Like a bear,
Sitting in a monkey's chair.
When the chair began to crack
All the fleas ran up YOUR back.

I was really enjoying being part of that chorus and part of that gang, all shouting and pointing. For once I felt I was a true part of the playground world. The girl leaped on to one of the seats in the shelter-shed and flattened herself against the wall. Suddenly, as I chanted and pointed, along with all the others, I remembered what it had been like a few weeks earlier when I was the one who was being chased, with other kids shouting, 'Witch! Witch! Witch!' as they ran after me. My arm flopped down at my side and I stopped chanting. If I had been a true hero I would have tried to rescue that girl who was hemmed in in the shelter-shed, but I was just too scared to try. I simply walked away.

You might think that these things – the things that happened to me and the things I saw happening to other people – might have taught me to be more sensible. No way! Though I no longer wanted to be a witch with a poisonous bite, I still wanted the everyday world to become marvellous around me. I still wanted to be the hero of some story. Day followed day in an ordinary real-world way, and then, suddenly, I had (once again) a chance to transform myself in storybook fashion. But (once again) it did not work out in the way I had hoped it would.

This time it began, not with a fancy-dress ball, but with a film that came to our local cinema. It was *The Jungle Book*, the story of an Indian boy, Mowgli, who, lost in the jungle when he was a baby, was adopted by wolves. Mowgli grew up among animals and learned to speak their languages, so that he could talk not only to wolves but to tigers, monkeys and snakes, as well. I loved that film. I was changed by it. Indeed, I loved it so much that I tried to make it come true for me in the everyday school-playground world.

At that time there were English children at my school – children who had been sent to live with New Zealand grandparents, so that they would escape the bombing of London. I stole part of their true story, stole part of Rudyard Kipling's invented story and twisted them into a story of my own. 'I flew out from London,' I told other children in the school playground, 'but the plane crashed in the jungle. I was found by wolves and I lived with them there in the jungle, learning to speak the language of the animals.' This wasn't just an invented story (I declared). It was true.

Things began slowly. I tried out this story on one or two children who told other children and my story spread around the school. Soon little groups began to challenge me once more. I did my best to prove that what I claimed was true. I invented a sort of mumbling, nonsense language which I tried out on passing dogs. When the dogs looked at me in astonishment I declared that they could understand what I was saying, but this only made the other children shout with laughter. I grew more and more determined to show them that I really belonged to the magical world of animals. What do animals do? They eat. What do they *eat*? I began eating grass and leaves and drinking from roadside puddles, just as some animals did, trying to prove I was truly linked to them. It was the only proof I could think of at the time.

Even when I began eating grass the other children at school were all far too sensible to believe my story.

But boys and girls began to come up to me in the playground bringing handfuls of leaves and berries. 'Eat this!' they would demand, thrusting something – a dock leaf or a dandelion – towards me and I would eat whatever they waved in my face. I had to. I remember how some leaves burned my tongue and how horrible some of the berries tasted. However, I did not hesitate for a moment. I found out, years later, that the teachers at school knew what was going on out in the playground, but none of them interfered, though for all they knew some of the leaves and berries I was eating could have been poisonous. Once again that school playground seemed to stretch itself out all the way between school and my home. 'Eat this! Eat this!' other children cried as we walked home, thrusting out their grass and leaves and berries, and I would chew and then swallow whatever they offered me.

Chasing a witch with a poisonous bite can become a little boring after a while and so can the sight of someone eating leaves and drinking out of puddles. But just as other children were growing tired of seeing me eat leaves I accidentally did something that excited them all over again. I ate a leaf without noticing something that other children were already well aware of. There was a caterpillar clinging to that particular leaf. If I had seen that caterpillar, I might have rescued it. Who knows? I might even have told the other children that I could talk caterpillar language. As it was, I just crammed the leaf into my mouth and ate it, caterpillar and all. Within a second other children were leaping around me screaming, 'Ugh! Ugh! She ate a caterpillar!' Well, I don't really blame them.

There was no way I could enjoy what was happening to me. Indeed I hated it. It was so different from what I had imagined it would be like when I began to invent my story. Certainly, I had not turned into the mysterious and wonderful creature speaking animal language I had imagined I might be. Instead, I had become a school fool, eating leaves and caterpillars and drinking dirty water – and it was all my own fault.

Troubled times seem to go on and on. But nothing, not

even a bad time, lasts forever. After a while, in spite of the caterpillar excitement, the other children lost interest in seeing me eat leaves. As for me, I fell silent. For many years I said nothing more about my magical powers. Instead, I began writing stories in little notebooks. I would go home and sit in my room scribbling tales about beautiful wild horses, and children who lived adventurous lives with pirates and gangs of outlaws. I had successfully woven my way into story-life after all, but I had to do that weaving shut away in my own room, just as I do today.

Trying to turn myself into a witch with a poisonous bite, or a child who could talk the language of animals, did not take up much of my school time. I suppose it was really only a matter of a few weeks here and there. However, whenever anyone asks me whether I enjoyed school or not, the first thing that I remember is trying out those impossible stories on other children who were all too sensible to believe me. And I also remember being part of the playground chorus tormenting that girl in the shelter-shed.

I learned a lot at school – I learned to read and write, and I learned the multiplication tables – things which I use every day. But I also learned how stories can work in the world. The odd thing is that nowadays, when I watch the news on television, it seems to me that heads of many countries are trying hard to make everyone else believe that they are the true heroes of the world's stories, and that other countries around them are ruled by villains. I haven't yet seen any prime minister or president eating grass... but who knows? They tell powerful stories and then have to prove them, so one of these days they might do just that.

Robert Swindells
Porkies

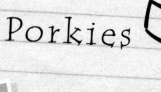

Mount Everest

ROBERT SWINDELLS was in the RAF for three years, then had a variety of jobs including shop assistant, clerk, printer and engineer. He trained as a teacher, then taught for eight years before becoming a full-time writer. He won the Children's Rights Workshop Other Award for *Brother in the Land* which also won the Children's Book Award. He won the Children's Book Award again for *Room 13* and, in the shorter novel category, for *Nightmare Stairs*. He won the Carnegie Medal for *Stone Cold* and the Angus Book Award for *Unbeliever*.

Robert Swindells

Porkies

Piggo Wilson was an eleven-plus failure. We *all* were at Lapage Street Secondary Modern School, or *Ecole Rue laPage* as we jokily called it. Eleven-plus was this exam kids used to take in junior school. It was crucial, because it more or less decided your whole future. Pass eleven-plus and you qualified for a grammar school education, which meant you went to a posh school where the kids wore uniforms and got homework and learned French and Latin and went on trips to Paris. At Grammar School you left when you were sixteen to start a career, or you could stay on till you were eighteen and go to university. *Fail* eleven-plus and you were shoved into a Secondary Modern School where you wore whatever happened to be lying around at home and learned reading, writing and woodwork. You couldn't get any qualifications and you left on your fifteenth birthday and got a job in a shop or factory. Not a *career*: a job.

One of the rottenest things about being an eleven-plus failure was that you knew you'd let your mum and dad down. *Everybody*'s parents hoped their kid would pass and go to the posh school. Some offered bribes: *pass your eleven-plus son, and we'll buy you a brand new bike.* Others threatened: *fail your eleven-plus son, and we'll drag yer down the canal and drown yer.* But grammar school places were limited and there were always more fails than passes.

It wasn't nice, knowing you were a failure. Took some getting used to, especially if your best friend at junior school had passed. You'd go and call for him Saturday morning same as before, only now his mum would answer the door and say, 'Ho, hai'm hafraid William hasn't taime to come out and play: he's got his Latin homework to do.' *William*. It was Billy before the exam. You'd call round a few more times, then it'd dawn on you that you wouldn't be playing with *William* any more. Grammar School boy, see: can't be seen mixing with the peasants.

Most kids took it badly one way or another, but it seemed to bear down particularly heavily on Piggo. The rest of us compensated by jeering at the posh kids, whanging stones at them or beating them up, but that didn't satisfy Piggo. What he started doing was telling these really humungous lies about himself. He'd stroll into the playground Monday mornings and say something like, 'Went riding Saturday afternoon with my grandad, bagged a wildcat.' He'd say it with a straight face as well, even though everybody *knew* he'd never been anywhere near a horse in his life and wildcats lived in Scotland. In fact if you pointed this out he'd say, 'Yes, that's where we rode to, Scotland.' Or we'd be listening to Dick Barton on the wireless and he'd say, 'My *dad*'s a special agent too, y'know: works with Barton now and then.' If you pointed out that Dick Barton was a fictional character he'd wink and tell you that was Barton's cover story. He couldn't help it, old Piggo: he needed to feel he was special to make up for everybody else seeing him as a failure.

Anyway that's how things were, and by and by it

got to be 1953. There was something special about 1953, even at Lapage Street Secondary Modern School, because of two momentous events which took place that year. One was the coronation of the young Queen Elizabeth at Westminster Abbey. 'My cousin'll be there,' claimed Piggo, 'she's a lady-in-waiting.' 'She's a lady in *Woolworth*'s,' said somebody: a correction Piggo chose to ignore.

The other momentous event was the conquest of Mount Everest. For decades, expeditions from all over the world had battled to reach the summit of the world's highest peak, and many climbers had hurtled to their deaths down its icy face. Finally, in 1953, a British expedition succeeded in putting two men on the summit. They planted the Union Jack and filmed it snapping in a freezing wind. The pictures went round the world and the people of Britain surfed on a great wave of national pride: a wave made all the more powerful because it was coronation year.

As coronation day approached, and while the Everest expedition was still only in the foothills of the

Himalayas, our teachers decided that Lapage Street Secondary Modern School would stage a patriotic pageant to mark the Queen's accession to the throne, and to celebrate the dawn of a New Elizabethan Age with poetry, song and spectacle. A programme was worked out. Rehearsals began. An invitation was posted to the Lord Mayor who promised to put in an appearance on the day, should his busy schedule permit.

We failures were excited, not by all these preparations but by the prospect of the day's holiday we were to get on coronation day itself, and the souvenir mug crammed with toffees every child in the land was to receive. I say *all*, but it would be more accurate to say *all but one* of us was excited. While the rest of us laboured to memorise a very long poem about Queen Elizabeth the First and hoarded our pennies to buy tiny replicas of the coronation coach, Piggo Wilson sank into a long sulk because he couldn't get anybody to believe his latest story, which was that Mount Everest had actually been conquered years ago in a solo effort by his uncle.

He'd tried it on Ma Lulu first. Her real name was Miss Lewis. She was the only woman teacher in our all-boys' school and she took us for Divinity, which is called RE now. On the day the news broke that Sir John Hunt's expedition had planted the Union Jack on the roof of the world, she was talking to us about the courage and endurance of Sherpa Tensing and Edmund Hillary, the two men who'd actually reached the summit, when Piggo's hand went up.

'Yes, Wilson?' We didn't use first names at Lapage.

'Please Miss, they weren't the first.'

Ma Lulu frowned. '*Who* weren't? What're you blathering about, boy?'

'Hillary and Sherpa whatsit, Miss. They weren't the first, my uncle was.'

'Your *uncle*?' She glared at Piggo. We were all sniggering. We daren't laugh out loud because Ma Lulu had two rulers bound together with wire which she liked to whack knuckles with. Rattling, she called it.

'Are you asking us to believe that an uncle of yours *climbed Mount Everest*, Wilson?'

'Yes, Miss.'

'Rubbish! Who *told* you this, Wilson? Or are you making it up as you go along, I expect that's it, isn't it?'

'No Miss, my dad told me. My uncle was his brother, Miss.' Sniggers round the room.

'What's his name, this uncle?'

'Wilson Miss, same as me, only he's dead now.'

'His *first* name, laddie: what was his first name?'

'Maurice Miss: Maurice Wilson.'

'Well *I*'ve never heard of a mountaineer called Maurice Wilson.' She appealed to the class. 'Has anybody else?'

We mumbled, shook our heads. 'No,' snapped Ma Lulu, 'of course you haven't, because there's no such person.' She glared at Piggo. 'If this uncle of yours had conquered Mount Everest, Wilson, *everybody* would know his name: it would have become a household word as Hillary has, and Tensing.'

'But Miss, he didn't get back so it couldn't be proved. Some people say he never reached the top, Miss.'

'Wilson,' said Ma Lulu patiently, 'two weeks ago I set this class an essay on the parable of the Good Samaritan. You wrote that you'd been to Jericho for your holidays and stayed at the actual inn.' She regarded him narrowly. 'That wasn't quite true, was it?'

'No Miss,' mumbled Piggo.

'Where did you *actually* spend those holidays, laddie?'

'Skegness Miss.'

'Skegness.' She arched her brow. 'Does Jesus mention Skegness at all in that parable, Wilson?'

'No Miss.'

'No Miss He does not, and why? Because Jesus never visited Skegness, and your uncle never visited Everest.' She sighed. 'I don't know what's the matter with you, Wilson: not only do you insult *me* by interrupting my lesson with your nonsense, you insult those brave men who risked their lives to plant the Union Jack on the roof of the world. Open your jotter.'

Piggo opened his jotter. 'Write this: *I have never been to Jericho, and my claim that my uncle climbed*

Mount Everest is another wicked lie, of which I am deeply ashamed.' Piggo wrote laboriously, the tip of his tongue poking out. When he'd finished Ma Lulu said, 'You will write that out a hundred times in your very best handwriting and bring it to me in the morning.'

We all had a good laugh at Piggo's expense, but an amazing thing happened next morning. Instead of presenting his hundred lines, Piggo brought his dad. He didn't look like a special agent, but nobody'd expected him to. We watched the two of them across the yard, but we had to wait till morning break to find out what it was all about. Turned out Piggo's late uncle *had* made a solo attempt on Everest back in the thirties and had been found a year later 7,000 feet below the summit, frozen to death. The climbers who found him claimed they also found the Union Jack he'd taken with him, which seemed to prove he hadn't reached the summit, but the story in the Wilson family was that Maurice had taken *two* flags, left one on the peak and died on the way down. The climbers had found his spare. The fact that nobody outside the family believed this didn't worry them at all.

Ma Lulu probably didn't believe that part either, but she was as gobsmacked as the rest of us to learn that Piggo's tale was even *partly* true. She apologised handsomely, cancelled his punishment *and* used our next Divinity lesson to tell us the story of Maurice Wilson's brave if foolhardy attempt to conquer the world's highest peak all by himself. We were a bit wary of Piggo after that, but taunted him slyly about his family's version of the outcome. He stuck to his guns, insisting that his uncle had beaten Tensing and Hillary by more than twenty years.

Our pageant came and went. The Lord Mayor didn't. He had another engagement but his deputy attended, wearing his modest chain of office. Some parents came too. Piggo's mum was one of them, which is how we found out she wasn't a Siamese twin as her son had insisted. On coronation day school was closed. There were very few TVs then, so most people listened to bits of the ceremony on the wireless. Most *adults* I mean. We kids had better things to do, like setting the golf-course on fire as an easy way of uncovering the lost balls we sold to players at a shilling each.

For us, the best bit of that momentous year came a few weeks later. The Headmaster announced in assembly that a local cinema was to show films in colour of the coronation ceremony, including the Queen's procession through London in her golden coach, *and* of the conquest of Everest, compiled from footage shot by expedition members, including the final assault on the peak and views from the summit. Pupils from schools across the city would go with their teachers to watch history being made in this stupendous double bill. There'd be no charge, and our school was included.

We could hardly wait, and Piggo was even more impatient than the rest of us. '*Now* you'll see,' he crowed, 'it'll show the peak just before those losers Tensing and Hillary stepped on to it and my uncle's flag'll be there, flapping in the wind.' We smiled pityingly and shook our heads, but he seemed so confident that as the day approached, our smug certainty wavered a bit.

It was at the Ritz, right in the middle of the city. A fleet of coaches had been laid on to carry the hundreds of kids from schools all over the district. Ours didn't arrive first. We piled off and joined a queue that curved right round the building. The class in front of us was from one of the grammar schools so we spat wads of bubblegum, aiming at their hair and the backs of their smart blazers. Red-faced teachers darted about, yanking kids out of the queue and shaking them, hissing through bared teeth, *'D'you think Her Majesty spat bubblegum all over Westminster Abbey: did Sherpa Tensing spag a wad from the summit to see how far it would go, eh?'* It made the time pass till they started letting us in.

They ran the coronation first. It was quite a spectacle, the scarlet and gold of the uniforms and regalia sumptuous in the grey streets, but it didn't half go on. We got bored and began taunting Piggo. 'Which one's your cousin then, Wilson: you know, the lady-in-waiting?'

'Ssssh!' went some teacher, but it was dark: he

couldn't see who was talking. 'Come on Wilson,' we urged, 'point her out.' Piggo made a show of craning forward to peer at the faces in the procession. There were hundreds. After a bit he pointed to an open carriage that was being pulled by four horses. 'There!' he cried, 'that's her, in that cart.' Just then the camera zoomed in, revealing that the woman was black. We shouted with laughter, and Piggo muttered something about having relatives in the colonies. As the camera lingered on her face, the commentator told us the woman was the Queen of Tonga.

The film dragged on. A great aunt of mine, who had a bit of money and owned the only TV in our family, had had people round on coronation day. Those early TVs had seven-inch screens, the picture was black and white, or rather black and a weird *bluish* colour, the image so fuzzy you had to have the curtains drawn if you wanted to see anything. Coverage had lasted all day, and my great aunt's guests had sat with their eyes glued to it from start to finish. *Get a life* I suppose we'd say nowadays, but it was the novelty: none of those people had seen a TV before. Anyway, I was thankful not to have been there.

The Everest film was a great deal more interesting to kids like us. Much of it had been shot with hand-held cameras on treacherous slopes in howling gales so you got quite a lot of camera-shake, but the photographers had captured some breathtaking scenery, and it was interesting to see mountaineers strung out across the snowfield roped together, stumping doggedly upward with ice-clotted beards. Another interesting thing was the mounds of paraphernalia lying around their camps: oxygen cylinders, nylon tents, electrically-heated snowsuits, radio transmitters and filming equipment, not to mention what looked like *tons* of grub and a posse of Sherpas to hump everything. Brought home to us how pathetically underequipped Piggo's uncle had been with his three loaves and two tins of oatmeal, his silken flag. Or had it been *two* silken flags? Underequipped anyway.

We sat there gawping, absorbed but waiting for the climax: that first glimpse of the summit which would silence poor Piggo once and for all, and he was impatient too, confident we'd see his uncle's flag and be forced to eat our words. It was a longish film, but presently the highest camp was left behind and we were seeing shaky footage of Tensing: 'Tiger,' the press would soon christen him, inching upward against the brilliant snow, and of Hillary, filmed by the Sherpa. We were getting occasional glimpses of the peak too, over somebody's labouring shoulder, but it was too distant for detail. There was what looked like a wisp of white smoke against the blue, as though Everest were a volcano, but it was the wind blowing snow off the summit.

Presently a note of excitement entered the narrator's voice and we sat forward, straining our eyes. The lead climber had only a few feet to go. The camera, aimed at his back, yawed wildly, shooting a blur of rock, sky, snow. Any second now it'd steady, focusing on the very, very top of the world. We held our breath, avid to witness this moment of history whether it included a silken flag or not.

The moment came and there was no flag. No flag. *There* was the tip of Everest, sharp and clear against a deep blue sky and it was pristine. Unflagged and, for a moment longer, unconquered. A murmur began in thirty throats and swelled, the sound of derision. 'Wilson you *moron*,' railed someone, 'where is it, eh: where *is* your uncle's silken flipping flag?'

Piggo sat gutted. Crushed dumb. We watched as he shrank, shoulders hunched, seeming almost to *dissolve* into the scarlet plush of the seat. Fiercely we exulted at his discomfiture, his humiliation, knowing there'd be no more bragging, no more porkies from this particular piggo. The film ended and we filed out, nudging him, tripping him up, sniggering in his ear.

We were feeling so chipper that when we got outside we looked around for some posh kids to kick, but they'd gone. This small disappointment couldn't dampen our spirits however. We knew that what had happened inside that cinema: the final, irrevocable sinking of Piggo Wilson was what *we*'d remember of 1953. We piled on to our coach, which pulled out and nosed through the teatime traffic, bound for *Ecole Rue laPage*. When we came to a busy roundabout the driver had to give way. In the middle of the roundabout was a huge equestrian statue; the horse rearing up, the man wearing a crown and brandishing a sword. Piggo, who'd been sitting very small and very quiet, pointed to the statue of Alfred the Great and said, 'See the feller on the horse there: he was my grandad's right-hand man in the Great War.'

Berlie Doherty

The Puppet Show

'My theatre's broken.'

BERLIE DOHERTY started writing seriously at university, where she was studying to be a teacher. She has twice won the prestigious Carnegie Medal, once for *Granny Was a Buffer Girl* – in which there was a whole chapter based on her parents – and once for *Dear Nobody*, the playscript of which won the Writers' Guild Award. *Daughter of the Sea* also won the Writers' Guild Award. Her other books include *The Snake-stone*, *Street Child*, *The Sailing-ship Tree*, *Tough Luck*, *Spellhorn* and *Holly Starcross*.

To Rita

Berlie Doherty

The Puppet Show

It began with Mickey and Minnie Mouse. My older brother, Denis, gave them to me for my ninth birthday. I had just left the little school in Meols at the time. I loved that school. In winter we had a real coal fire in the classroom, and when it grew dark the flames would flicker shapes and shadows on the walls until the light was put on. You could hear the sea from the yard. In the autumn we gathered chestnuts and leaves from the monkey woods round the school and brought them in to decorate the walls and windows. Some children hardened the chestnuts in vinegar and made holes in them, then threaded them with bits of string for conker fights in the playground. I liked to line mine up on my desk, admiring the way they gleamed like brown eyes. At the end of the day we used to run home along the prom, with the gritty sand whistling round our bare legs, and if there was time we'd play out till dark.

But the autumn term in the year of my ninth birthday had hardly started when the parish priest told my parents that I should be going to a Catholic school, and persuaded them to take me away from there. So I had a long journey by bus to a large flat school in the middle of a modern housing estate. There was a plaster statue of a saint in every classroom. Our room had the Virgin Mary in a blue dress, and she seemed to be watching us all the time with her sorrowing eyes. Occasionally the sickly smell of chocolate drifted in through the windows from the nearby Cadbury's factory, mingling with the smell of boiling cabbage or fish from the kitchens.

By the time I started there, nearly halfway through the autumn term, friendships had already been made. I was much too shy to talk to anyone, and nobody talked to me. I used to stand in the windy playground with my back against the railings and watch all the children running and shrieking and wonder how there could be so many children in one place, and how they could all know each other. I wished I could squeeze through the railings and run back home. When Mr Grady blew the whistle at the end of playtime the children all froze like the statues in the classrooms, and then at his second whistle they walked absolutely silently into class rows. There wasn't a child in the school who wasn't afraid of Mr Grady. His face was cold and hard and white, and I don't think I ever saw him smile.

One day he caught me reading in a lesson. I was supposed to be doing Arithmetic. I felt his hand coming over my shoulder and too late, he snatched the book away from my grasp and held it up. I was ice-cold with fear. The whole class watched him as he walked with the book to his desk. He had been known to beat children with his cane until they bled. He sat on the edge of his desk and drew a pile of exercise books towards him. Then he rooted through them and drew one out. It was mine.

'One day,' he said to the class, 'this girl will be a writer.'

But I did not feel proud or happy that he had said

that. I felt afraid, and ashamed. I hung my head and didn't look at anyone.

Our class teacher was Miss O'Brien, who had auburn hair like a fox's back. Her lips were bright red and shiny, as if she was always licking them wet, though I never saw her doing it. I longed to be noticed by her, but she always seemed to be in a dream, gazing out of the window as she taught us, somewhere far away. And around me, the children in the class giggled quietly and passed notes to each other, and shared secrets. They all seemed to be going to each other's houses for tea or to birthday parties. I was outside it all, just watching.

When my own birthday came around, in November, there was no point having a party. There was no one to invite. So it was a special treat when my brother arrived home unexpectedly, especially as he brought me two presents. 'I couldn't decide which one to get you,' he said. 'So I got them both.'

They were glove puppets, one of Mickey in a blue smock, one of Minnie in a pink smock with a yellow bow painted on her shiny black rubber head. They both had round beaming cheeks and huge smiling eyes. The heads were hollow, so I could put my hand inside them and bunch up my fist in the cheeks. The smocks covered my hands. I could make the heads bob about and look round and talk to each other. Everybody laughed when I made funny voices and made the puppets talk. I found I could say anything I liked with these puppets on my hands, and nobody minded. I could tell Jean, my sister, that her hairstyle was horrible, or her new dress looked like a sack of potatoes, and as long as I said it in Mickey's voice she thought it was really funny.

'Gee, I guess I'll just have to smarten myself up for you, Mickey,' she drawled, putting on an American accent. When my mother lit up her cigarettes, which I hated, I would put my Minnie puppet on and pretend she was coughing, and Mum would dab her cigarette out. 'Sorry Minnie,' she would say, 'I forgot about your bad chest.'

It was a kind of magic.

I took Mickey and Minnie to school, and sat with my hands under my desk, tucked inside them. Usually in class I sat in absolute silence, never daring to speak or even to put my hand up, even if I knew the answer to any of Miss O'Brien's questions. Her voice droned on in the hot classroom. I looked round. Everyone was looking fidgety and sleepy. Suddenly my hands seemed to shoot up of their own accord, with Mickey and Minnie bobbing about in the air.

'This place could do with a bit of livening up!' said Mickey.

'Don't you know any jokes, Miss O'Brien?' said Minnie.

Only it wasn't Mickey and Minnie, it was me. The children sat up in their desks and stared at me, and Miss O'Brien stood with her mouth wide open. And then an amazing thing happened. She answered back in a Donald Duck voice.

'Oh boy!' she squawked, pouching out the side of her cheek like a balloon, 'there's two darned mice in my classroom!'

After school, everybody wanted to have a go with the puppets. I looked round till I saw the most popular girl in class, Dorothy Ewers, who had a mass of curly hair. 'That one,' Minnie said, 'that girl with bubbles all round her face. She's my best friend.' Dorothy flushed with pleasure and grabbed Minnie from my hand.

'Well, I'm Mickey's best friend,' another girl, Maria Stephens said. 'If you let me play with him you can come to tea tomorrow.'

As soon as we got to her house Maria put on a purple ballet dress and pranced round the garden, leaving me sitting with my glove puppets making comments like, 'Whoops, there she goes, Mickey. Did you see that fairy?' 'No, but I saw a flying elephant, Minnie,' making Maria giggle breathlessly. When she finally stopped, red-faced and gasping, she said, 'You can wear my ballet dress now, and I'll have a go with Minnie and Mickey.' It was a dream come true, and I floated round her rose beds like a princess, snagging the foamy material on thorns while Maria beamed at me.

The next day I was invited to Dorothy Ewers'

house. We had chocolate marshmallows for tea. Dorothy sat playing with Mickey and Minnie while I tucked in. I had only had a chocolate mallow once before in my life, and my dad had cracked open the chocolate shell on his forehead as a joke. I did it at Dorothy's, expecting everybody to smile. Her father stared at me for a long time and said, 'Who is this bad-mannered child, Dorothy?' I was mortified. I nearly burst into tears, but I remembered the magic. I grabbed Mickey off Dorothy's fist and made him say, 'Who is this grumpy man, Minnie?' And they all laughed, even Mister Ewers.

Suddenly I had more friends than I could cope with. Everybody wanted a go with Mickey and Minnie. I was bribed with licorice sticks and chocolate marshmallows, offers of invitations to birthday parties, of goes on scooters and with yo-yos. It was a dizzy time of popularity, a social whirl of outings to tea, and Mickey and Minnie got grubbier, the smocks got torn, and finally, the smiling rubber faces split in half.

As if a balloon had popped, the fun fizzled away.

The cheeky comments didn't work without the puppets. I wasn't special any more; nobody shared their playtime biscuits with me. And without my puppets, my shyness came back. I stopped speaking in class. I started fainting in assembly. Nice Mr Jenkins used to scoop me up and carry me out to the playground for fresh air. Word got round that I could make myself die and come back to life again. The children looked at me as if I had some strange, mysterious power, and kept away.

During this time another new girl arrived. She used to stand at the other end of the yard staring across at me. Nobody played with her. I knew how she felt, but I looked away, pretending not to see her. I didn't know how to go up to her and say, 'Can I be friends with you?' I could have said it in Minnie's voice, if she'd still been alive. Because that was the way I thought about them. My puppets had died, really died, and I was in mourning for them.

And then one day I had a wonderful idea. I would make more puppets. I ran home after school and begged my mum for some material, and she gave me an old pair of curtains. I cut out two shapes of a princess in a ballet dress and sewed them together, and turned them inside out. Then I tried to stick my hand inside. It was too small for my hand, but I could just squeeze it over three fingers. It was all right. She could bow, she could turn, and I could make her sing. I sewed yellow wool on to her head for hair. That made her tighter still, but it was still all right.

I made a prince, being careful to cut out larger shapes this time. He was so big that he flopped right over my fist and his velvet smock covered my arm up to my elbow. It was fine. He could bow and he could kiss the princess and he could speak in a loud, deep voice. I went to bed dreaming about my puppets. Before school I ran next door and asked Mrs Berry if she had any old frocks I could use, and she gave me some glistening sequins to put in my princess's hair, and some blackout curtains left over from the war for a witch's cloak. 'I've lost one of my lovely fur mittens,' she said as I was leaving. 'Would you like the other one to make a cat with? Here's some pipe cleaners for his whiskers.'

At the end of a week of frantic cutting out and sewing and glueing, my bedroom was a mess. My sister Jean, who shared it with me, threatened to make me sleep in the WC in the back yard. I had an array of glove puppets lined up on my bed, all different shapes and sizes, some with the stitches showing and gaps in the seams where the cotton had broken. I thought they were utterly beautiful. I had a prince and princess, a clown with a red button for a nose, a witch, a cat, an old man with white wool hair and beard, a giraffe that had started off as a dog, a baby with a safety pin holding a handkerchief nappy round its middle, and a teacher who was supposed to look like Miss O'Brien, with orange wool hair and bright red lips. I made up voices for all of them, and then – well, this is where my ambitions carried me away – I decided to make a theatre for them.

I would write a play, and they would be the actors. I would tour it round the school. I would be popular again.

I don't know how I had the courage to advertise my show. I was such a shy child most of the time, without my Mickey and Minnie props. But I wrote out posters and stuck them in the classrooms, and arranged with the teachers to do my show at the end of the week. They all agreed. It was Monday. I had four days to build a theatre, write a show, rehearse the actors and learn the lines.

I wrote feverishly, a speaking part for every character, howls and hiccups for the baby, miaows for the cat, and something like a horse's whinny for the giraffe. The story was a mixture of *Punch and Judy*, *Cinderella* and *Lorna Doone*, which I'd just heard on the radio. I had to make sure that no more than two actors were on stage at the same time, or I would run out of hands. I don't think I slept all week. I worked by torchlight while Jean grumbled and muttered and snored and grumbled again. I begged some shoeboxes at the local Woolworth's store and carried them home on my bicycle. Back to the cutting and glueing. Out came the paints. And – the final touch – curtains on a piece of string stretched across the stage. The show was ready.

It was raining on Friday. I waited at the bus stop hugging my theatre in my arms, trying to keep it dry. The puppets were in my schoolbag on my back. I stood with my eyes closed reciting my lines and nearly missed the bus. Somebody's umbrella spiked through a corner of the theatre. The wet curtains dripped dismally. Still, the show wasn't due to start until after the last playtime. There was plenty of time to dry everything out.

I fainted in assembly again that morning, in a drowning rush of black and red swirls and dazzling sparkles, of overwhelming heat and icy cold. When I came round Miss O'Brien was dabbing my face with a cold flannel and the new girl, Rita Chrisp, was staring down at me, her eyes huge and blue and full of concern. Miss O'Brien tipped my head between my knees and sent her away.

Nobody else spoke to me all day. I couldn't face the Friday boiled fish at dinnertime. My posters taunted me wherever I looked. I'd misspelt one of the words. Puppet Theater, I'd written. Someone had crossed it out and corrected it in red ink. I squirmed miserably. I wanted to tear the posters down and forget that I'd ever even thought of doing the show. I wanted to run home and hide in my bedroom. The afternoon dragged on. Playtime came. And after play – the show. I went to look at my theatre again. Someone had trodden on it. One of the sides had come right off. And I knew, then, that I couldn't go on with it. The puppets were ridiculous; I could see it now. They didn't look anything like the characters they were meant to represent. They were just bundles of old rags. And I couldn't remember a word of the script. I sat on the floor and sobbed my heart out.

I was aware that someone had come into the classroom. I wiped my eyes on the sleeve of my cardigan.

'I came to wish you luck.'

It was the new girl, Rita. She'd never spoken to me before. I don't think she'd spoken to anybody. I looked up at her. She had the bluest eyes I've ever seen in my life.

'What's the matter?' she asked.

I burst into tears again. 'I can't do it,' I sobbed. 'It's stupid. I wish I'd never said I'd do it. I want to go home. I feel sick. Everybody's going to laugh at me.'

'I won't laugh at you,' Rita said.

'My theatre's broken.'

'I've got some glue in my desk.'

'I hate it. It's a mess. The puppets are horrible.'

'I like the princess,' Rita said. She knelt down and squeezed her fingers into the princess's head. 'Where'th my handthome pwinth?' she lisped. She shoved her fist inside the Prince and made him bow. 'Oh my, ain't you cute!'

I started giggling. I hopped the cat up to her and purred.

The show was a disaster.

The glued theatre collapsed halfway through the first act, and Rita ran up and lay on the floor next to me, holding it together. I got my lines mixed up and brought the witch on stage too early, so the prince fell in love with her instead of the princess. The clown's nose dropped off. The entire audience yelled, 'That's Miss O'Brien!' when I brought the teacher on stage. 'Oh no it isn't,' the real Miss O'Brien said from the back row. 'Oh yes it is!' they roared. And I realised then that they didn't hate my show at all. They were enjoying every disastrous minute of it, and so was I.

Rita helped me to carry my theatre to the bus stop. She came round after tea and we played out under the lampposts. That night I shoved the theatre under my bed and lay staring up at the ceiling. I'd written a play. My first play. And I'd got a friend. A real friend. I turned off the light and floated into a deep, blissful sleep.

Jeremy Strong

A Thoroughly Idle Boy

She also liked to play Kiss-Chase. Wow!

JEREMY STRONG has been a headteacher, teacher, strawberry picker and a jam doughnut stuffer! His first book was *Smith's Tail*, published in 1978. Since then he has written many books including five stories about *The Karate Princess*, and the books about Nicholas and his family including *My Mum's Going to Explode!* His three Viking stories – *There's a Viking in my Bed*, *Viking at School* and *Viking in Trouble* – have been made into a hugely popular television series. Jeremy won the Children's Book of the Year Award for *The Hundred-Mile-an-Hour Dog*.

Jeremy Strong

A Thoroughly Idle Boy

I'm not proud of the title of this story. It was what a teacher wrote on one of my school reports, and it was perfectly true. I came across a whole bunch of these reports recently, when I was giving my filing system a spring clean, even though it was midsummer. (See – I'm still idle!) Anyhow, I have used some of the comments from the reports throughout this piece, and they made me start thinking about how it all started. How did I become a 'thoroughly idle boy', amongst many other crimes?

I think it probably began on the day I discovered I was on my own in the world, alone. It was going to be me **v** the rest of the world.

I realised this when I was six, coming up for seven. We had just started a new year at infant school. I was in the oldest class, what you would call Year Two. The teacher was preparing her new register on the first day of term, checking names, addresses, telephone numbers and birth dates. Like everyone else I knew it all off by heart, everything – everything except my birth date. I had no idea when my birthday was. I knew it happened sometime during the year, but I didn't know when. It just wasn't important in my world.

So Mrs G, my new teacher, checked my name and address and so on.

'Jeremy Strong, what's your date of birth?'

'I don't know.'

And everyone burst out laughing. Even Mrs G was trying to hide a smile.

The children all around me were children I had known for over a year. Many of them were my friends, I thought. Now they were all laughing. I began to think that if my friends sniggered because I didn't know my date of birth then what on earth would happen if I didn't know the answer to something important, like all those awkward things we kept on learning about?

I am fairly certain that it was from that time that I

became more and more of a loner. I didn't trust other people. I didn't trust adults because you never knew how they would take things. I didn't trust children for much the same reason. I'd got into trouble earlier because of other children. You know how it happens. You're five years old and you say something like 'Poo!' (If you are five, and the year is 1954, then 'Poo' is a pretty bad word – oh yes!)

Your friend laughs. He thinks it's funny too, so you say 'Poo!' again. Then all of a sudden your friend has his hand up and he's saying: 'Miss Cox! Miss Cox! Jeremy Strong said "Poo!"'

And Miss Cox – tall, slim, beautiful Miss Cox, who I adore, says: 'Oh, Jeremy!' in that tone of voice.

And the thing is, does the shame of being told off by Miss Cox make me stop saying 'Poo'? Of course not! In fact I think I'll say something else. Oh yes! 'Bum! Knickers!'

Oooh, I know,

'Milk, milk, lemonade;

Round the corner chocolate's made!'

You see, at five years old I had discovered *two* things:

1. If you say rude words people snitch on you and you get into trouble.

2. If you say rude words people are shocked. People pay attention to you. People listen. It's a kind of fun, and since I always seemed to be getting into trouble, I might as well have fun doing it. So, 'Bum, Poo, Knickers to everyone!'

Hmmm, I wonder... I wonder if I was a loner because nobody wanted to be friends with someone who was always in trouble?

So, at almost seven, I was a loner, but there are great advantages to that. You are left in your own world, and if you have any imagination at all – and most children have – you start inventing things, like your own games and your own conversations. If nobody wants to talk to you and you want to have a conversation then you have to invent all the bits of it. You talk to yourself, and to the trees and plants and animals.

So I would wander around, stare at the flowers in

the school garden and say: 'Hello Little Busy Bee! Bzzz, bzzzz, bzzzz. You're very busy. Do you get hot with all that work? Do you get sweaty armpits? No, you haven't got arms – so, do you get sweaty legpits? You'd have six sweaty legpits! Urgh, what a stink! Do bees use underleg deodorant?'

Then I'd suddenly realise that two or three children were standing beside me, grinning like monkeys and laughing.

'You're mad!' they'd say. 'You talk to bees!'

To tell you the truth, I still do! I often talk to myself out loud when I'm out walking and I'm thinking about a story, or I'm considering an important meeting I am about to have. I rehearse what I might say, what the other person might say, and so on. (And no, I'm not mad. People often do things like that inside their head. It's just that I do it out loud too.)

'Jeremy's result should be much higher than this...'
So there I was at primary school, on my own for the most part, and things were slowly getting worse.

Every month we were tested – on Comprehension (understanding), Composition (writing a story), Spelling and Maths. Then once a term we were given a big test on everything the teacher had ever taught us. Phew. Hard work. (And I don't like hard work.)

My marks got steadily worse. I started off getting marks like 98 out of 100, which were pretty good, but by the time I was in Year Six I was getting 59 out of 100. I was so scared of telling my parents I reversed the two digits and told them I'd got 95! They were over the moon – until they found out. Big Trouble!

'I just misread it,' I lied.

'You liar!' my parents said, telling the truth.

'He should adopt a more adult attitude to his work.'
Life was not easy, and I made everything much harder for myself insisting on doing things my way. (It's embarrassing to report that it's still a bit of a problem even now. I do like to be in control.)

But don't teachers say funny things sometimes? I mean, that little bit up above – my teacher put that on my report when I was eleven. Eleven! How can you be adult when you're eleven? Even my dad thought it was daft.

Anyhow, all this was going on when something staggering happened to me. The clouds parted and sunshine burst upon my life. The house directly opposite from us was sold and new people moved in. There was a husband, who was a teacher, his wife, their two girls and a baby boy. It was nice to have a new family across the road, even though their oldest child was younger than me, and a girl. (You know how it is: up to the age of mid-teens or so you never lower yourself to speak to younger children unless they are your own brothers and sisters.)

However, although the oldest girl, Susan, *was* younger than me, she was a vision of sunlight. She had long, long blonde hair that danced about her head, a smile that made her eyes crinkle, and a sprinkling of cheeky freckles. We would meet up in the fields, usually with other friends around too, and we spent a bit of time together. That's all it was. I didn't think of her as a girlfriend – after all, she was younger than me. But I liked to be near her and despite her being younger she was no pushover. She answered back – and how. She also liked to play Kiss-Chase. Wow!

It's a good game, Kiss-Chase, and Susan could run fast. (Although most of the time she ran slowly because she liked to be caught!)

I could run pretty fast myself.

And so could my friend, Colin.

So there we were, playing Kiss-Chase, with me running down one side of a building, Susan up ahead, and Colin running along the other side of the building.

He couldn't see me.

I couldn't see him.

When we reached the corner of the building—
BAMM!

We collided, banging our heads together. I went sprawling on to the grass and my face hit a large, rusty padlock that was just lying there. My cheek was split open just beneath my eye and blood went everywhere.

It was pretty impressive.

I got up, holding my cheek together, blood streaming down my face, and went off home, with Susan dancing attendance. She kept asking if I was all right. Yeah – no problem!

Then my mum saw the cut and whisked me off to hospital. I ended up with three stitches. Ouch – that was the bit that hurt!

But, when I got back from casualty, Susan thought I was the bee's knees. I had been so brave. (Good thing she hadn't seen me at the hospital!) I was her hero. So I got to kiss her. All Colin got was a banged head. (He was too young for her, anyhow. He was only ten.)

Yes, Susan was good fun.

'He cannot hope to succeed like this...'
Then, after the sunshine, the big black clouds. My parents decided to move house. We went to a bigger, smarter house, about three miles away. It was only three miles, but it was enough for Susan and I to lose touch. I was plunged into The Dark Years.
Somehow I had managed to get to Grammar School,

and that was where my problems really started. They began with TR, (which probably stood for Tyrannosaurus Rex). TR was repeating his first year. Heaven alone knows what he had done (or probably *hadn't* done) to achieve this honour. It meant that not only was TR a year older than anyone else in the class, but he had a grudge too. He decided to take it out on me, and he got his mates in the year above to help out.

Break-time became a daily hell. A typical day would see me penned up inside the coal bunker, while the older kids lobbed lumps of coal over the top of the wire cage. Or maybe it would be a straightforward bit of roughing-up.

What TR and his mates didn't know was that when they weren't looking I would copy their homework answers into my own books. Only once did a teacher get suspicious, and after that I made sure that when I copied the answers I always made two or three changes so it seemed like my own work. What a horribly sneaky child I was! But it was lovely to feel that I was getting my own back on them.

However, I was really on my own. I didn't feel that there was anyone in the world who I could talk to, or who would understand or who quite simply cared. I guess that sounds a bit melodramatic, even pathetic. But if *you* have ever been in that state yourself – and remember, this went on for years – you will know what I mean. All you want is one person who will listen. It doesn't even matter if they can't do anything about it – but to have one person with whom you can share without fear of ridicule or being made to feel like – well, it's your own fault anyhow – that is all you want. But there was nobody. (Not even the busy bees!)

'He runs away from anything he dislikes.'
My willingness to do anything at all at school gradually evaporated away and my reports grew worse. Everyone was on my back. Everyone knew I could do better. Was I going to? No. As long as all those everyones out there were making the decisions and telling me what I should be doing I made sure I did the opposite. The adults would say: 'The only person you're

hurting is yourself.' And of course they were so right; I knew that. A report at the time said: 'He runs away from anything he dislikes.' You bet I did! Who wouldn't?

'He fears no punishment...'
The school tried everything to make me work, and at this particular school 'everything' actually only meant three things: detention after school, the slipper, or the cane. The more they tried, the less I responded. The more they talked at me, the more I crawled inside my own shell and hid.

My mother told me recently that she always knew when I was coming home from school with a bad report because I would be clutching a bunch of flowers to give her, in the hope of putting her in a good mood. 'Heaven alone knows where you got them from,' she added. 'You probably pinched them from the Headmaster's garden!' (She was right.)

Then, about three years after moving, an amazing thing happened. I bumped into that blonde girl again. By this time her hair was even longer and her smile made me feel like I was in an Easter Egg factory.

We started seeing each other, and this time it was serious. Suddenly I had that one person who would listen, who cared.

Even better was the fact that I now had someone I wanted to impress. I had long ago given up on wanting to impress my parents – that task just seemed too difficult. But Susan – she *wanted* to be impressed. And as for the rewards I might get from her – oh boy! She didn't play Kiss-Chase any more – she couldn't be bothered to do all that running away bit. Susan just stood still and waited!

'He is prepared to work hard in certain subjects...'
I didn't exactly turn over a new leaf at school, but I did begin to improve at the things I liked – music, art, writing, English. Some of the masters even stopped wanting to kill me and became cautiously pleasant. (Me likewise.)

It's little wonder I enjoyed writing. When you write stories you are out there on your own, inventing your own world. I've always loved that kind of escape, not to mention the control, the power! (The only time people have always done what I've told them to do has been in stories.)

There was one sport I enjoyed at school, and that was Cross Country Running. I enjoyed it for three simple reasons.

1. I was good at it.

2. It got me out of afternoon school.

3. You ran for a long time, on your own. You were not part of a team. You just went out there and ran, alone with your own thoughts and nobody to bother you.

So what happened in the end? I managed to finish Grammar School well enough to go on to further education. I carried on writing for myself. I carried on seeing Susan. In fact I still see her today because we got married. (And that was twenty-eight years ago.)

As I said at the beginning of all this: I am not proud of what I did (or rather *didn't*) do at school. I was pretty stupid in many ways, and as my teachers kept telling me, the only person getting hurt was myself. I guess that overall I must have spent about eleven years of my life battling with teachers. At the time I hated most of them.

So what did I do when I finally grew up and needed a job? *I became a teacher*! You've got to laugh, haven't you?

Of course, the story can't end like that, and it doesn't. All the time I was teaching I was also writing, writing, writing. Some stories got published, and then some more. Eventually I left teaching and now I just write.

I found one other comment on a report. This was during The Dark Years, and it was next to my exam result for English.

'The high mark was largely due to a successful poem. I doubt whether he could "pull it off" like that every time.'

Jenny Nimmo
Dormitory Nights

'Ooooh! Whatever is it?'

JENNY NIMMO has been an actor, researcher, floor-manager and script editor for children's television. Her first book The Bronze Trumpeter was published in 1975. The Snow Spider – the first title in a fantasy trilogy – won the Tir na n'Og award and the Smarties Grand Prix. Her other novels include The Witch's Tears, The Owl Tree, winner of the Smarties gold medal for younger children, Griffin's Castle, and for older readers Milo's Wolves, and The Rinaldi Ring, which also won the Smarties Grand Prix.

Jenny Nimmo

Dormitory Nights

It all began with a white elephant; not the sort that weighs a ton and has a trunk and two big ears. The white elephant I'm talking about is something that is of no use to its owner, but extremely desirable to somebody else.

Every summer the Girl Guides held a fête at the boarding school where I spent most of the year. I wasn't a guide myself, because when they had their meetings I was always doing something else. Like reading.

One hot day in May, when I was ten, the guides set out their stalls on the lawn in front of the school. My friend, Barbara, and I began to stroll around, having a go at the games and buying sweets and cakes. Or rather Barbara bought the sweets while I clung to the two shillings in my pocket.

Barbara, like me, was not a guide because she, too,

was always doing something else when the guides held their meetings. Only in Barbara's case it was usually tennis, or hockey or netball. She was a tall girl with brown pigtails and very long legs, and she was brilliant at sports.

I came to a halt beside a long table. A sign at the back of the table read: White Elephants. Piles of old books were stacked behind chipped cups, china animals with lost ears and tails, broken necklaces and all sorts of ancient and battered toys. In the middle of the toys lay a pink plastic violin. It was only sixpence. Today it would be two and a half pence. So you can understand what a bargain it was.

For a few seconds I hesitated and then out came my money. First I bought a book and then the violin.

Barbara watched me in amazement. 'What d'you want that for?' she said, tapping the violin. 'You could have bought loads of food for sixpence.'

I didn't have a reply. We were always hungry because we had to take violent exercise at least four times a day, and snacks weren't allowed. So food would have been more sensible. Except that Matron always confiscated any food she found in the dormitory, and then doled it out after tea, a tiny bit a day, so that most things like cakes, were stale by the time you got to the last slice.

'I should get your money back,' Barbara advised. 'Look, that thing has only got two strings.'

This was true, but I held on to the violin. 'It might come in useful,' I said weakly. I had no idea, at that moment, how extremely useful my new white elephant would be. How it would provide hours of entertainment but set me on a collision course with the grim school matron, and to the very brink of being expelled.

You wouldn't think a small pink violin could be responsible for all that, would you? Well believe me, it could. And it was.

As soon as I'd bought my book and my violin, I wanted to take them up to the dormitory. It was forbidden to visit the dormitories until after tea, but I couldn't carry my new possessions round the fête while

I spent my last few pennies trying to win something in one of the tricky games the guides had devised.

Barbara agreed to come upstairs with me. She wanted to hide the piles of food she'd bought in her tuck box. We left the garden and nipped into the school by a side door. The back stairs led to the sanatorium and the linen room. This was where Matron and her assistants hung out, so we decided to use the main staircase that led up from the hall. It was a very grand affair with twirling newel posts and delicate gleaming bannisters. It mounted to a wide landing where portraits of the Principal's ancient forbears hung, and then it curled round and ended right in front of the staff-room.

On that particular day even the staff were enjoying themselves out in the sunny garden, so, sliding across the highly polished floor, we raced to the passage that led to our dormitory; Cherry Dormy, as we called it.

We had almost reached the door when our luck ran out. A chilling voice called, 'And what are you two doing?'

We swung round. There was Matron, standing only

a few metres behind us. She was dressed all in white, except for her thick legs, which were encased in pinky-brown stockings. Her face was white too, and her eyes stared straight through you; the irises were so pale they were no colour at all, just a black circle with a dot in the centre. I called her 'Polar Eyes' because that's just what she did. She polarised you.

Barbara spoke first. She said, 'We bought some things at the fête and wanted to put them in our lockers.'

'Why?' Matron came towards us.

'Because our things are heavy and we wanted to play some of the games.' I held up the pink violin, hoping to divert Matron's attention from Barbara's bags of sweets.

It worked. 'And what do you propose to do with that?' Matron glared at the violin.

'Play it,' I said.

'Not in the dormitory.'

'Oh, no. I just want to keep it in my locker.'

'Very well. I'll give you two minutes, and then I

want to see you outside.' She was a fresh air fiend and hated seeing anyone indoors unless they were asleep, washing or working.

Meekly, we answered, 'Yes, Matron.'

It took me only a second to get my possessions into my locker. But Barbara had to hide her sweets under the false bottom of her tuck box. The tuck boxes were kept beneath our beds, and although they were originally intended to hold food, (tuck) our boxes only contained toys and books. However, Barbara had a large and understanding father. Knowing how much his daughter loved food, he had cunningly inserted a false bottom in her tuck box so that illicit food could be hidden there safely.

That night, I lay in bed listening to my friend chewing her forbidden sweets and I began to wonder why I'd bought a pink violin instead of food. We went to bed very early, long before the sky was dark, and long before we were tired enough to go to sleep. After lights out we weren't allowed to talk or read, and there was nothing to do but lie in bed and think. The suppers we had never filled me up, and I thought of all the cakes and iced buns I'd seen on the Girl Guides' stalls.

Ten girls slept in Cherry Dormy. There were four beds on each side of the room and two at one end. At the other end, long windows reached from floor to ceiling, making the rooms freezing in winter and baking when it was sunny. We had cherry-coloured blankets, and the long thick curtains were also cherry-coloured. There were no carpets and the old floorboards creaked horribly whenever we got out of bed. This was also forbidden, except to go to the lavatory.

Beside each bed there was a small cupboard, or locker. Some of us kept torches in our lockers, because, if you were brave enough to take the chance, you could read under the bedcovers.

I didn't feel like reading, and yet I wanted entertainment of some sort. I opened my locker and took out the pink violin. I plucked the two strings. Plunk! Plunk! I turned the tuning pegs and made a higher note: Plink! Plink!

'What's that?' someone said.

I didn't answer. Instead I tapped the side of the violin: Tap! Tap! Tap!

'Sounds like a mouse,' whispered Amanda Samuels, two beds away from me.

I blew into one of the sound holes behind the fingerboard. This made a brilliant sound, like the wind howling down a chimney.

'Ooooh! Whatever is it?' squeaked Mary Harvey. She was a small, timid girl and easily frightened.

I was beginning to enjoy myself. This was much more fun than lying in bed thinking about food. I turned the tuning peg tighter and this made a lovely creaking sound, like an old door opening very slowly.

Mary Harvey shrieked and put her head under the covers. The school was very old and ghosts were not unheard of.

Unfortunately, Barbara could see me in the light that filtered through the thick red curtains. 'Jenny, it's you, isn't it?' she said.

'Yes,' I confessed. 'It's my white elephant.'

Barbara giggled. And then everyone began to

giggle. Everyone except Amanda Samuels who whispered, 'Shut up, everyone, or we'll be caught.'

'No, we won't,' said Barbara. 'Go on, do some more, Jenny.'

So I did some more. I made hoofbeats, squeaking doors, footsteps, howling wind, ghostly whispers, a rocking-chair and an eerie elfin tune. These sounds were just crying out for a story and I found myself providing one. It began with an old woman, all alone in a little old cottage in the middle of a wide, dark moor. A storm raged outside, but through the claps of thunder, the little old woman could make out the unmistakable sound of hoofbeats. A horse neighed. Footsteps approached the cottage. A knocking could be heard. Knock! Knock! Knock!

'The little old woman was too afraid to move,' I said. By this time I had forgotten to whisper. 'A latch was lifted – click – and the door swung open – Creak! Creak!' I turned the tuning peg.

'And guess who...' I stopped as the dormitory door was suddenly flung open.

Quickly, I dropped the violin behind my locker, but it was too late to lie down.

The light snapped on and Matron stood on the threshold. 'Who was talking?'

It was obvious. I was still sitting up in bed. Matron glared at me, her eyes even icier than usual. 'Jenny Nimmo, you know the rules. Don't let me catch you again.' She swept out.

For a moment there was absolute silence, and then Mary whispered, 'Finish the story, Jenny, please!'

'Please! Please! Please!' whispered nine voices.

How could I disappoint such an appreciative audience? I retrieved the violin and then waited a few moments.

It was very unfair of Matron to wear rubber-soled shoes. You could never tell when she was closing in on you. However, she did carry a large bunch of keys, clipped to her belt, and if you were lucky you could sometimes detect a slight jangling sound when she was about.

When I was quite sure that no jangling was going on

outside the door, I began again. Matron must have been hanging on to her keys to keep them quiet because, without any warning, the door flew open again.

I just managed to drop the violin behind my locker before Matron reached the light switch. But, once again, I was caught sitting up in bed.

'Nimmo, bring your mattress!' Matron barked.

We all knew what that meant. If you were caught breaking the rules more than once in a single night, you had to sleep in a classroom away from everyone else. You were allowed a mattress and one blanket. Nothing else.

As I dragged my bundle out of the room I could see nine heads lying, as still as stones, on nine pillows.

Sleeping in an empty classroom was no fun. It was freezing cold, for one thing. There were no curtains and moonlight made a shadowy forest of the desks and chair legs. Sleep was out of the question, so I told myself stories until I was so tired I had to close my eyes.

Next morning, Matron wouldn't let me go to

breakfast until everyone else was downstairs. I was late, of course, and had to eat the last kipper. It was cold, dry and bony, and it put me off kippers for life.

My friends kept asking how I managed to keep my spirits up in the dark and empty classroom. I told them that I had entertained myself and, that night, they wanted to hear my new stories.

'Tell us a nory,' said Mary, 'you know, a story with noises.'

'No,' I whispered. 'I'm not going to talk after lights out.'

My resolve lasted a week. In the end I found that I was just as keen to tell a nory, as the others were to hear one. So out came the pink violin and I began.

This time Matron was so quick she had turned on the light before I had time to hide the violin.

'Give me that,' she said in a chilling voice.

I handed over my violin.

'Now get your mattress and follow me.'

I wasn't going to be given a second chance. Off I went to the cold classroom, to spend another night shivering and scaring myself with terrible stories. Before I fell asleep I vowed never again to talk after lights out.

This wasn't an easy vow to keep. Not when I was surrounded by pleading whispers, and when my head was full of stories that were just aching to be let out. So, eventually, I gave in.

My pink violin had been confiscated, so I had to make do with other effects. I used hairbrushes, slippers, pencil boxes, rubber bands, combs with sweet papers wrapped round them, anything, in fact, that made an interesting sound. I suppose I must have been a very silly child, or just reckless. I should have been aware that all these things made more noise than the violin. But it was such a challenge. I couldn't resist it.

It was inevitable that Matron would hear me. In she came. On went the light, and there I was, sitting up with my sound-making instruments spread over my cherry blanket.

An angry flush spread across Matron's white face. She turned dark pink. In a choking sort of voice, she said, 'Put on your dressing-gown and slippers!'

This was new!

I put on my dressing-gown and slippers.

'Now, go and stand outside the Principal's office.'

This was unheard of. Awful. The end. I was about to be expelled.

Quaking with fear, I shuffled out of the dormitory and down the main staircase. From the landing above, Matron watched my every step.

I waited in the draughty hall for about half an hour before the Principal's door opened. She was a small woman with white hair and spectacles, but I was scared stiff of her. Her face was sad and solemn, and she always gave the impression that she was deeply offended by any bad behaviour. As she listened to my stuttered confession, I felt she had the power of life and death over me.

When I had finished the Principal gave me one of her long, disappointed stares. 'It seems that you can't be trusted,' she said in a stony voice. 'I'm very disappointed in you. Obviously you can't go back to the dormitory. The other girls need their sleep, even if you don't. You'll have to sleep in the sanatorium, and you'll stay there until we decide what to do with you.'

My heart sank. But at least I wasn't being expelled. Yet.

That night I carried my clothes and belongings along to the sanatorium. I spent seven nights alone in the long dreary room where white sheets covered the empty beds, and a horrible smell lingered round the huge medicine cabinet. It was so bleak and white and dreadful my brain felt numb and I couldn't even think of any stories.

At the end of the week something happened. A small girl called Mary-Jane Patterson, caught chicken-pox. She had to be isolated, so I was allowed to leave the sanatorium. I wasn't to go back to my dormitory, however. This time I had to sleep in the linen room. It was a tiny room right at the back of the building. I'm sure it was haunted. Every night I would get a cold tingle down my spine and feel someone was in the room, watching me. Sleeping in that tiny room was worse than anything.

At last I was allowed back to the dormitory. I had

learned my lesson, so they thought. And so I thought. But after a while the whispers started up again.

'Tell us a nory, Jenny!' 'Go on!' 'Please!' 'I'll give you my sweet ration!' 'You can have all my sequins!' 'Please tell us a nory!'

'Better not,' whispered my wise friend, Barbara. 'This time you really will be expelled.'

But I couldn't help myself. I got out all the bits and pieces I need for the best nory I would ever tell: combs, brushes, boxes, tins, sweet papers, rubber bands and a torch. This nory would be *son et lumiere* – sound and light. It began in the same way as the other nories, with the little old lady in her lonely old house, and it ended with her climbing up the chimney in order to escape the monster that had burst into her house; a monster with flashing eyes and a terrible growl.

The noise I made must have been considerable, but no one caught me. No one crept up, listened then flung open the door. This time I had got away with it. I could hardly believe it.

In the morning, after the bell had woken us up,

Matron did her rounds, checking that we were awake and getting dressed. When she came to our dormitory she stood and stared at my face for what seemed like an age, and then she said, 'You were talking after lights out, weren't you?'

I could hardly confess. And yet did I dare to lie? How did she know? I became aware that the other girls were staring at me. Some looked scared, others surprised. Barbara looked slightly anxious.

'Don't bother to lie,' said Matron with a nasty smile. 'It's written all over your face.'

What did she mean?

She marched me over to the mirror. I looked at my reflection. My face was covered in spots.

'But...' I said faintly. 'They're just spots – it doesn't mean that I talked after lights out.'

'Children who break the rules always get their comeuppance,' said Polar Eyes. 'Off to the sanatorium with you. You've got chicken pox.'

I should have guessed. Polar Eyes was a witch!

I spent a miserable three weeks in that awful, white,

smelly room. Mary-Jane had recovered and moved out, so I was all alone. No one was allowed to visit me and I could only get my 'fresh air' while everyone else was in lessons. All contact was forbidden. Sometimes, Barbara would come round to the courtyard under my window and wave. But the area was out of bounds and she didn't dare stay long enough for a chat.

When I was finally out of quarantine I was allowed back to the dormitory, and to all my friends. They had been starved of stories for so long they were desperate for a nory, 'a really scary one,' said Mary.

I was ready for them. I hadn't been idle during those terrible weeks of confinement. 'I've written a play,' I said, and handed out sheets of paper. 'If you all learn your parts we could do the play on the last night of term. It would be official, so we wouldn't be breaking the rules.'

It worked. Nearly every night for the rest of the term, the girls in my dormitory burrowed down their beds with their torches and learned their lines. We got permission to do the play on the last night of term and it was a great success. Barbara had the leading role and I directed and did all the sound effects.

I can't say I *never* told another nory, because that wouldn't be true. But I waited until I was in a different dormitory. It was at the top of a very creaky staircase and this time I could hear Polar Eyes approaching long before she reached the door. I was always ready for her, with eyes tight shut and not a single sound effect in sight.

Bernard Ashley

'Ashley, Sit There!'

'Cracked the pavement?'

BERNARD ASHLEY was a headteacher for many years before becoming a full-time writer. His first novel *The Trouble With Donovan Croft* won the Children's Rights Workshop Other Award. His novel *Dodgem*, which he serialised for television, won the Royal Television Society Award for best children's programme. His novels for older children include *Tiger Without Teeth*, *Johnnie's Blitz* and *Little Soldier* and for younger children *Dinner Ladies Don't Count* and *King Rat*.

Bernard Ashley

'Ashley, Sit There!'

There was only one free place in the classroom. It was at the front, one half of a double desk, with its own lift-up lid but a shared hinged seat. If one of us stood up to answer a question – and in those days you had to stand up to speak to the teacher – the other had to stand as well.

'Ashley, sit there.'

Ashley! I'd never been 'Ashley' in London. In London I was 'Bernard,' or 'Bernard Ashley' if I was up to mischief. But never 'Ashley'.

It was the first day of the new evacuation, and we were in Preston, Lancashire – my mother, my younger brother, Michael, and me – because she hadn't let us go off to be evacuated with the school. In the first 'blitz' we'd gone to Hertfordshire but had come home when things quietened down. Now Mrs Gritton, a neighbour who was already evacuated to Preston, sent back addresses of others who would take people in. It was a paying business, seaside landlady money in a small Preston house not far from the abattoir.

Our father later said it was the worst eight minutes of his life, the incident that sent us away. He was a London fireman called out on the fire appliance to a 'shout' at the top end of Flaxton Road, where a big bomb had dropped. And this was where we lived, and where we were, home from school, at the time. But it wasn't us who 'caught a packet', our family good fortune was someone else's tragedy. When the fire engine turned the final corner Dad saw that we were OK, and they had to go further up Flaxton Road to the devastation; number 127 was still standing, and we were safe in our Anderson air raid shelter in the back garden. But that was it! Another 'blitz' had started, and we were packed off out of London on the first available train.

'Ashley, sit there.' The first morning in an alien school. From that moment in Preston I've known what it feels like to stand in front of a class of kids looking at someone as if they've come from Mars. I know something of what it must feel like to be Rwandan or Vietnamese or Somalian in Britain. But in my day evacuees were from London and Londoners were Cockneys, and Cockneys were nothing but thieving toe-rags. Shop doorways sometimes said it: *No evacuees* – the way shops today say *Only two school kids at once*. All of which amounted to a first, unpleasant impression – although I later made good friends and the stereotypes on both sides gave way to truth.

Anyway, I sat there – next to the prettiest girl I'd seen, after my London sweetheart Maureen Vickery. And it could have been the emotion of being wrenched away from my life so far, from my bike and my comic collection and my books and toys – and Maureen Vickery – but I fell immediately in love. Her name was Clare: blonde, serious, with a pretty nose, a beautiful mouth and teeth like a Hollywood film star. And aloof. She dead set her shoulder against me and got on with her work.

It was a big class. Forties and fifties were common class sizes anyway, anywhere, but in wartime they were bigger still. Even the male teachers too old for 'active' service in the army, navy or air force were called up for other war service, which is why my father was a London fireman. Also, many young female teachers went into the ATS, the WRAF and the WRENs (female army, air force and navy personnel), so those teachers who were left had big classes which were often ruled by fear of the cane, the ruler and the slipper.

Miss Gibbs, my new Preston teacher, was strict like that. As well as my own home, what I suddenly missed about London was the gentle kindness of Mrs Nunn, my teacher in south London. Even she wasn't above a knuckle rap with a ruler – you had to make a fist and take it – but it was never thin edge on, and she never sent anyone to the head for the sort of brutal caning he could dish out. If you were in Mrs Nunn's class you were protected from the harsh world of school by someone rather like a 'firm but fair' grandmother.

Doh-ray-me-fah-soh-lah-te-doh. That was singing in Preston. In London we sang *songs* – *Pedro the Fisherman* who was always whistling, and *The Lincolnshire Poacher* – tunes going with a cheerful, uplifting beat. But in Lancashire a ruler rapped the special blackboard on which the Tonic Sol-Fa was painted, and you had to hit the note the ruler commanded as Miss Gibbs jumped it up and down. She would suddenly point at you and command, 'Fah!' I didn't know *Fah* from a fish supper – and a vocal shot in the dark always missed the musical mark and got a twist of disdain from her. This was *music*? To them it was, and the local kids had had years of hitting the right notes, which only showed how London brats had no proper education.

But the crucial examination for a new kid happens in the playground.

'Where you from?'

'What team?'

'Good at '"Kingy"'?'

'Can you fight?'

'Where's your dad?'

'You seen a bomb?'

I had seen a bomb, lots of them, or the effects they had – and saying so led to my first big mistake. A gang of boys told me about a bomb that had fallen in Preston town centre and cracked a paving slab – a small incendiary bomb, the sort dropped to start fires. And I scorned it. *Cracked the pavement?* A boy who had seen a whole street devastated by a land mine, who had a camp on a bombed site, who'd seen the fires of the burning London docks changing the sky to Hell – I had to sneer at a cracked pavement.

And so they hated me. Which was a lesson to learn – more valuable than any of Miss Gibbs', or even Mrs Nunn's – never make someone else's experience seem inferior.

The beautiful Clare wasn't in on this – and since boys and girls did different things in school as well as in the playground, she wasn't in on my punishment, either. Even in Elementary Schools the sexes were separated for certain lessons like Needlework and Woodwork. In

Lancashire the correct uses of saw and chisel were taught, and you stood to attention on your side of the bench to receive instruction and then followed it a step at a time. Discipline was on the fierce side of strict with all those sharp tools around; it was military, frightening, a long way from having a chat while you worked thin wicker round thicker wicker in London, making baskets for Christmas presents.

The morning after the bomb sneer, the woodwork teacher, an older man too old to 'serve', had to suddenly leave the room – probably suffering from a weak bladder.

'Tools… down! You, Coe, to the front.'

Colin Coe, one of the bomb-cracked pavement boys, went out to the front, cautiously because it could have been for anything. He might have planed when he should have rasped and a clip round the ear could be waiting for him.

'Stand at the front, lad. You boys, you touch nothin' an' you say nothin'. While you, Coe,' – he drew out the name on a long 'oh' sound – 'you report t'me any boy who moves or speaks while I'm out.'

Coe looked round the room with an eager face. He surely would! The man went out and the class held a rigid parade ground stillness and silence. We stood to attention measuring our breaths in case they made our cheeks move. Nobody twitched a muscle – in London somebody would have done a modest blow-off. It was the perfection of a silent tribute, because no joker dared voice his wonder about what the man had gone out for. *Two minutes an' it's number one, five minutes an' he's doing number two, ten minutes an' he's doing Miss Gibbs!* That would have been London – but this was Lancashire splendour, for those who admire the power of fear.

After a bit the man came back. We all looked at his flies, of course.

'Coe...' Long drawn out again. 'Did any lad move or speak?'

'Yes sir.'

It was a lie. We could have been our own toy soldiers lined up.

'Who?' The man's old tortoise eyes flicked around the room.

'Ashley, sir.'

Now a few muscles moved, small smiles at the benches. And Ashley's inside turned over with a great squirt of fear.

'Coom out, Ashley.'

'I didn't, sir,' I started protesting as I walked out to the front.

'So, ye've brought your London ways with you, have you, lad? Don't they know down south the meaning of *meaning*?'

With a shake starting to come on me I watched him reach for his cane, a straight stick without the curved handle, which sat along an inside edge on his teacher's bench. He picked it up and bent it, put a flex into it.

'I never, sir, honest, I never said anything...' My voice was on an upward curve through *soh* to top *doh*.

'When we say *don't talk* in Lancashire we mean *don't talk*. What do we mean?'

'But I never—'

'*What do we mean?*' He brought the cane down on his bench with a crack like a firing squad.

'Don't talk, sir.'

'Then you'll have to learn that, Ashley. Up!'

He poked my right hand with the cane. I held it up, and out, the way boys did in London. I'd never had it before, but like every boy and girl in every school I knew the procedure.

Crack! The cane came down across my palm in a swift whistling strike. Yelp! It hurt like hell and the pain seared in like a poker burn. But I hadn't flinched back from taking it and I didn't snatch my hand away to comfort it between my legs. I kept it there for the next while my heart thudded scared blood. And, I don't know, but he might have been impressed by that – because he dismissed me. No more. Just the one.

'That's a warning, Ashley, that we mean what we mean in this part of the world.'

My hand burned on through the day. But what brought the tears in the end – when I saw my brother

Michael in the playground – was self pity and outrage at the attack on me.

But wouldn't Clare be impressed? I'd had the cane, I was one of the bad boys. And a martyr – wouldn't she feel sorry for me, the way girls in London sometimes wept for a boy who'd been punished? I hoped someone in the class might say what had happened in Woodwork, but they didn't so I tried to keep my hand open on the desk so that she could see the weal. But she took no notice, and I had to get through the rest of the day just feeling abused – and thanking God we didn't have a handwriting lesson because holding a pen gave me the shakes.

Even more than ever I wanted something to do with Clare. I can't remember that I dreamt about her, but I know I thought about her a lot. I did want some personal contact with my pretty desk partner, but she wanted none. In London, Kiss-Chase was a soft and sexy alternative to 'Kingy' but they didn't seem to play it up here. So I was reduced to secondary contacts. Like, when we were sharing a hymn book, me holding one half of the book, Clare holding the other, instead of keeping it upright I would press it down flat and away from us. She didn't want it at that angle and she'd bring it back up again from her side: a silent, hymn singing tussle. But I could feel her force, through the book. It was as pathetic as that! Or if I went up and down holding the bench seat, she had to do it, too.

My father kept in touch from London. He wrote a letter every week – and sent an instalment of a Robin Hood story printed in a paperback magazine, two columns of small print to the page, stapled with a paper cover.

They became important to me – contact with my father in London and stories that told of a hero exiled from his own home by a wicked oppressor, the Sheriff of Nottingham; who was just like me, driven from London by the evil Adolf Hitler. Stories do this. They give us comfort and strength from knowing that we're not the only ones ever to have been in our situation. It's reassurance and encouragement, because although not all fiction ends happily, it often holds hope.

As the weeks went by things got better at school – with the boys. Perhaps it was the caning, or my being good at 'Kingy', the playground game of the moment. This was a sort of ball 'it' and I was good at it; not so much at the throwing but at the dodging of the hard ball. I was often the last to be cornered with everyone else on the hunt. We had a rag or handkerchief wrapped round our right fists and we could defend ourselves – punch away the ball – with it; which was small, a tennis ball 'core' most often, just the perished black rubber inside. I got into the best 'Kingy' game and that carried a certain status.

Also, the kids on the estate where I lived all walked to school at the same time (no 'school runs' in cars then), so there were friends to be made, which happens once people are seen as people and not labelled by race, religion or some geographical divide. Lennie Bamber was a good mate. He lived across the road from me in a house that backed on to the railway line, where we'd sit on top of the sleepers that were his back fence and watch the trains go by; some of them hospital trains filled with wounded troops on stretchers.

Meanwhile in London my father was injured. It was nothing too serious, a wrenched knee where he'd slipped fighting an oil fire in the docks. But it meant that he couldn't be an active fireman until the swelling went down and he could get full movement back into the leg. So he came to Preston on leave, with orders to report to the local hospital for physiotherapy. It didn't stop him from taking us to a local fair and going on the Moon Ride, nor to Blackpool on a day trip and riding the Big Dipper, Dad sitting up at the front with his walking stick. His sick leave was a sort of wartime holiday for us, although school was still on and I was adapting to Lancashire teaching. The disappointment was that Clare didn't seem to be getting any warmer towards me.

Sadly, all holidays come to an end. Soldiers on leave go back to their units, airmen and women to their airfields, and sailors to their ships. And, with Dad's knee better, he had to go back to London to face the air raids again. Firemen, policemen, air raid wardens and civil defence, they all had to be out under the bombs while the others were in their shelters, and we knew the dangers of that. The death rate among fire fighters was horrendous – Churchill's 'heroes with blackened faces'. Next time for Dad it might not be a wrenched knee but a wall falling on him, or a floor collapsing, or being blown to flesh and bone by a direct hit.

So it was a sad day, that last Friday, when Mum gave us the only day off school we'd ever had without being at death's door ourselves. Dad's train would leave at some time after five in the afternoon, so we went for a last picnic and play in a local park; a desultory affair, as miserable as the solitary monkey in a cage that lived there. We played a game of hide-and-seek – when I wanted never to find my father so he wouldn't have to go back – and we couldn't swallow much of the picnic because we were too choked. This smiling-too-hard, bright-eyed dad was leaving us today to go back to the war. This might be the last time we ever played with him.

At the end of it we went back to the house to pick

up his suitcase and go with him to the station to see him off. As we were walking for the bus the school was coming out; and we were still in Cintra Terrace when Lennie Bamber came running along the opposite pavement. He saw me, crossed the road, and came running through us – without a word, as if he didn't know me. And as he ran through he thrust something in my hand, didn't break step, gave me something and went running on: something small and secret that I clutched in my palm before quickly shoving it in my pocket.

'What's that you've got there?' my mother asked.

'Nothing.'

'That boy gave you something, in your hand.'

I showed her my empty hand.

'The other one, in your pocket.'

She wasn't being unpleasant, prying for its own sake, but she was more upset than any of us at what we were doing, saying goodbye to Dad – so she was making something out of nothing just for the sake of it, passing the awkward time. Now she used emotional blackmail.

'Come on,' she said, 'let's have a look. Let Dad share it.'

So I couldn't refuse. I was dying to see what it was myself, but not right then, thank you. I took my hand out of my pocket and opened the palm. It was paper, folded over and over into a sort of cube.

'That's a note,' Mum said.

'Yeah,' I said nonchalantly, going to put it back in my pocket.

'Well, let's read it! Let Dad check the spellings!'

Her look, on this unhappy day, told me I had a duty to brighten it with whatever sport was going. So I opened the note.

The paper was longer than it was wide, with a rough side and a smooth, three thin sheets joined in a vertical way by lines of perforations. And the message was written in pencil, on the rough side. We all read it together, silently.

Dear Bernard, it said, *I love you. Do you love me?* That was the first sheet, along the bottom of which ran a line of green print on the shiny side: *NOW PLEASE*

WASH YOUR HANDS. This note was on school lavatory paper – the sort we had before tissue.

'Ooh!' said Dad.

'Wow!' said Mum.

'*Who?*' said Michael.

I stayed silent, eyes bolting, reading on.

Shall we go out together? Shall we go up to the park? NOW PLEASE WASH YOUR HANDS.

And the finish – *All my love*, with Cupid's heart pierced by an arrow dripping not blood but kisses, which formed the name of – Clare!

Clare!

I didn't hear what people were saying, I was out of it! Clare loved me! The one day I hadn't gone to school and she'd missed me – and gone into the girls' lavatories to write me a love letter!

Shooting stars! Exploding bombs! It takes two to *feel* in love, so now I really was in love! Official! I floated to the bus stop, deaf and blind to the others and their questions, this trio of sadness – and my solo joy.

My solo *guilt*. Because at the station just before the

train left, the train taking my father back to danger and possible death, saying goodbye for what could be the last time, he hugged us all and kissed us. And he cried, and Mum cried, and Michael cried – and I tried to cry. But I couldn't. In all their grief I was so happy.

Which was when I first discovered how complicated life can be – a lesson of growing up that some unfortunate kids are born knowing.

So, Clare was my sweetheart for a few weeks – until the Friday that Mum had a letter from Dad saying that the bombing in London had stopped and we could go back. Which we did – a bolt home on the morning train the next day. Living in someone else's house had been hardest of all on my mother; preserving the peace, sharing the kitchen, keeping tabs on our rations, and she was packed before Friday's school was over.

So we went – and I never said goodbye to Clare nor ever saw her again.

'Didn't you chuck her first?' a boy asked me recently.

'No, there wasn't time. I didn't know her address to

write to, and there were few phones in the houses then.'

'Well,' the boy said, 'that means *officially* you're still going out with her.'

In that case I'm two-timing, I suppose.

Malorie Blackman

Jessica's Secret

My ears rang. My heart pounded.

MALORIE BLACKMAN was a database manager and systems programmer before becoming a full-time writer. *Hacker* won the W H Smith's Mind Boggling Books Award and the Young Telegraph Children's Book of the Year Award. *Thief!* won the Young Telegraph Children's Book of the Year Award and *Pig-heart Boy* won an UKRA Award. *A.N.T.I.D.O.T.E.* won the Stockport Children's Book of the Year Award. *Noughts & Crosses* won the Lancashire Book Award and was declared the outright winner of the 2002 Children's Book Award. Her books for younger readers include *Whizziwig*, which was made into a popular BBC Television series.

Malorie Blackman

Jessica's Secret

Emma never warned me. She never said a word. So I found out the hard way that Jessica was a bully. It only took two or three days in my new class to realise it. None of the other girls spoke to her – except Sarah. Even the boys gave her a wide berth. But me? I didn't know any better. As the new girl in an old class I was desperate to make friends. And I was only too aware that all the other girls had their best friends and their best groups and their best gangs already sorted out. Mid term was not the greatest time to start a new school – to say the least. Emma was given the task of looking after me but I wanted to make friends with everyone. And Emma never warned me.

'Hi, Jessica,' I smiled hopefully.

She looked friendly enough. Long, blonde hair pulled back into a tight ponytail. Ice blue eyes and a straight line of a mouth. She wore pink nail varnish too. Okay, so it was chipped and peeling, but she still wore it. That was more than my mum would let me do.

Jessica looked me up and down and didn't answer. Alarm bells started to sound but they were way off in the distance.

'Hi, Jessica,' I tried again, my smile broader this time. Maybe she hadn't heard me the first time.

'Malorie isn't it? What kind of name is that?'

'I like my name.' I told her. The scorn in her voice wasn't quite enough to stifle my response. Almost, but not quite.

'What school were you at before?' asked Jessica.

I told her.

Jessica turned to Sarah standing next to her and sneered, 'Get her! Doesn't think much of herself, does she?'

What'd I said? I'd answered her question and told her the name of my old school. What was wrong with that? The alarm bells were getting closer, louder. Sarah smiled at her friend before turning to me, her light brown hair fanning out as she whipped her head around, her cat-green eyes glistening with dislike. Jessica turned back to me, her face a mask of deep scorn. The class was only half full of the lunchtime stragglers but they were all silently watching, like a cinema audience who knew that a good bit was coming up.

'How well can you fight?' asked Jessica.

I frowned, sure I'd misheard her.

'How well can you fight?' Jessica repeated impatiently.

I shrugged. What was I meant to say to that?

'Hit her, Sarah.'

All the hopes and thoughts and alarm bells in my head stilled at that. It was like I'd stepped out of myself and stepped back to watch what was going to happen next. I turned to Sarah, still wondering what I'd done. She wasn't going to hit me just because Jessica said so, was she? I'd never done anything to her. She had no reason to hit me.

Sarah drew back her fist, then threw it forward with

her whole weight behind it. I tried to jump away but I backed into a desk. Sarah's fist thumped into my shoulder. If I hadn't moved, it would've been my face.

Dad's words rang in my ears. 'Don't let anyone push you around, Malorie. If someone hits you, hit them back.'

But I didn't want to. I'd never had a single fight in my previous school. Not one. When I was six, one boy had spat at me and told me to go back to the jungle, but even that didn't lead to a fight.

And I didn't want to fight now. But I had no choice. Shocked at what I was suddenly caught in the middle of, I pushed her back. Sarah drew back her fist and this time I had nowhere else to move to. She punched me full in the face. Sparkling lights flashed and danced before my eyes. My ears rang. My heart pounded. My face felt like I'd been picked up and slammed into a wall. That was all it took. Still seeing stars, I flailed around wildly, trying to hit Sarah even though I couldn't really see her, through the lights still bopping before me. I tried to move around her and away from the desks to give myself more room. Sarah hit me again. A swift punch to my stomach. I doubled over, holding my stomach and rushed at her, head-butting her in the stomach. Blood poured from my nose, splashing down on to the floor in small pools like scarlet raindrops.

Sarah grabbed me by my hair, pulled my head up and hit me again. I sunk down on to the floor, grabbed her leg and bit as hard as I could. Her pained scream wasn't much but it was better than nothing. My body wasn't hurting any more for some strange reason. Maybe because all I could think about was hurting Sarah the way she was hurting me. I pulled at Sarah's legs, toppling her over. Mistake. She kicked out with both legs, one of her feet kicking me in the shoulder.

We both scrambled up. Sarah hit me. And hit me. And hit me.

And all I could think was, 'Don't cry... don't cry...'

'That's enough,' Jessica said at last.

My shirt was sticking to me, not with sweat but with blood from my nose bleed. The only part of me that was hurting were my eyes, which were stinging horribly.

Don't cry, Malorie. Don't cry.

'You're a useless fighter,' Jessica said, shaking her head.

And she turned to walk out of the classroom. The others in the class silently parted to let her pass. She didn't hurry, she strolled without a single backwards glance. And that was worse than Sarah wiping the floor with me. I was nothing. Not worth looking at, not worth rushing for, not worth anything. Jessica left the room at the same unhurried pace. I turned away from her, hating her.

'Come on,' said Sarah softly. 'I'll help you get cleaned up.'

It took a few moments to realise she was talking to me. Sarah tried to take my arm, but I angrily shrugged her off.

Don't cry, Malorie.

'I want to help, okay? Come on. I'll help you wash the blood out of your shirt,' said Sarah.

She led the way out of the classroom and to the girls' toilets. No one else came with us. My eyes were still stinging, but that was nothing compared to the rest of my body now. Every part of me hurt. My nose, my cheeks, my stomach, my chest, my shoulder. For some strange reason, my ears were hot. Had she hit me on the side of my head or was I just filled with burning shame at being such a useless fighter that my whole face, including my ears were on fire?

Sarah got some toilet paper and wet it, before rubbing it over the many blood stains in my white shirt. All she did was smear it but I couldn't trust myself to speak without breaking down so I said nothing.

'I'm sorry about that,' Sarah said as she held another piece of toilet paper to my nose to try and stop it from bleeding. 'Jessica does that to all the new girls. I'm sorry. Every girl in the class has had to fight me at some time or another. She just does it to see how well they can fight. She's the best fighter in the class and I'm the second best. She just did it to see how good you were. She'll leave you alone now. I'm so sorry.'

Sarah carried on apologising and rubbing away at my shirt as I tipped my head back, swallowing the blood that gushed down my throat like I was some kind of thirsty vampire. I was proud of myself though. I hadn't cried. Not one tear. Not one.

'I'll get you, Jessica. You just see if I don't.' I consoled myself with that one thought, playing it over and over in my head like a spell. And the more I thought it, the more real, the more likely it got. Jessica may've been a better fighter than me but I was going to get her if it was the last thing I ever did.

Over the next few months, Sarah and I actually became friends. Not close friends. Not like me and Pauline and Emma and Suzanne, but friends nonetheless. Even Jessica and I had the odd conversation. But only when she spoke to me first. I didn't avoid her, but I didn't seek her company either. The fight was over and done with. Yesterday's news. Or so I thought. I really believed I'd put it all behind me.

But the first day back at school after the Easter holidays taught me differently.

Emma, Suzanne and I were playing French skipping

in the playground when Pauline came rushing over to us.

'Where've you guys been? I've been looking for you all morning. Guess what?' Pauline said, her velvet brown eyes sparkling with delight.

'What?' asked Emma, annoyed at having our game interrupted.

'I found out something about Jessica's family during the holidays,' said Pauline.

'What?'

'It's a secret about Jessica's mum and dad,' Pauline whispered.

French skipping was forgotten. We all huddled together, sensing a secret juicy enough to keep us licking our lips for a week.

'Come on then,' I prompted. 'Let's hear it.'

And Pauline told us all about Jessica's mum and dad. And we were shocked, appalled. I'd never in my wildest dreams thought that sort of thing happened outside nasty horror films. It never happened in real life – and certainly not to the parents of a girl in my class.

'I don't believe you,' I told Pauline when she'd finished.

'I swear it's true,' Pauline said indignantly.

'How did you find out then?' asked Emma, just as sceptical as the rest of us.

'Jessica's mum and my mum are cousins,' Pauline replied.

'You never told us that before,' said Emma.

'Would you admit to being related to Jessica?' said Pauline.

And she had us there.

'Is that really true?' I asked, still not quite sure whether or not to believe it.

'Every word,' said Pauline.

We all stood in silence as we considered exactly what Pauline had just told us. It certainly explained why Jessica was the way she was.

'Go and get everyone to come over here,' said Suzanne.

'Why?' I asked.

''Cause we've got something to tell them,' said

Suzanne, her eyes gleaming.

'The boys too?' asked Emma.

Suzanne mulled this over for a moment. 'No, just the girls.'

'You didn't get it from me – okay?' said Pauline.

'Don't worry,' said Suzanne.

Suzanne, Emma, Pauline and I spent the next five minutes desperately trying to round up as many girls in the playground as we could before the bell sounded. We had at least twenty and probably closer to thirty around us by the time Jessica wandered over to find out why such a large crowd was gathering.

'What's going on?' she asked with a frown.

She didn't stand a chance.

'We know all about your mum and dad,' Suzanne said at once. And she shouted out Jessica's secret at the top of her voice for everyone to hear.

Like I said, Jessica didn't stand a chance. Her face collapsed like wet newspaper. Tears immediately streamed down her face. Her shoulders sagged, her whole body drooped like a deflated balloon. We all stood watching her with undisguised hatred and satisfaction and as Jessica looked around for a friend, she could tell exactly what we were all thinking. With a sob, she turned and ran.

'And that's what I call getting my own back,' said Suzanne viciously.

Others in the crowd around us murmured their agreement. Jessica had hurt too many people, too many times to have any friends in the crowd. Even Sarah stood with us.

I stood there, watching Jessica run away, her face buried in her hands, thinking, 'We shouldn't have done that. That was so mean. Too wicked.'

But part of me thought, 'Good! Serves her right. Now she knows what it feels like to be hurt.'

But as I watched her disappear around the corner from us, I realised something. Far, far worse than being bullied was to become a bully myself. It was never going to happen. I swore there and then that I'd never, ever do that again.

Michael Morpurgo

My One and Only Great Escape

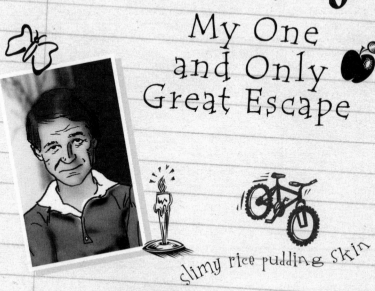

slimy rice pudding skin

MICHAEL MORPURGO is the author of over sixty books for children including *The Butterfly Lion*, winner of the Smarties Prize, the Writers' Guild Award and currently being made into a major motion picture. *The Wreck of the Zanzibar* won the Whitbread Award and was the IBBY Honour Book of 1998, *Kensuke's Kingdom* won The Children's Book Award, as did *Out of the Ashes*. His other titles include *The Dancing Bear*, *Farm Boy*, *Billy the Kid*, *Toro! Toro!* and *Cool!* Michael and his wife, Clare, established Farms for City Children and were awarded the MBE in recognition of their services to youth through this organisation.

Michael Morpurgo

My One and Only Great Escape

I still think of the house on the Essex coast where I grew up as my childhood home. But in fact it was my home for just four months of every year. The rest of the time I spent at my boarding school a whole world away, deep in the Sussex countryside. In my home by the sea they called me Michael. In my boarding school I was Morpurgo (or Pongo to my friends), and I became another person. I had two distinctively different lives, and so, in order to survive both, I had to become two very different people. Three times a year I had to make the changeover from home boy to school boy. Going back to school was always an agony of misery, a wretched ritual, a ritual I endured simply because I had to.

Then one evening at the beginning of the autumn

term of 1953 I made up my mind that I would not endure it any longer, that I would run away, that I would not stay at my school and be Morpurgo or Pongo any more. I simply wanted to go home where I belonged and be Michael for ever.

The agony began, as it always began, about ten days before the end of the holidays – in this case, the summer holidays. For eight blessed weeks I had been at home. We lived in a large and rambling old house in the centre of a village called Bradwell-juxta-mare (near the sea). The house was called 'New Hall' – *new* being mostly seventeenth century, with lots of beams and red bricks. It had a handsome Georgian front, with great sash windows, and one or two windows that weren't real windows at all but painted on – to save the window tax, I was told. House and garden lay hidden and protected behind a high brick wall.

Cycling out of the gate, as I often did, I turned left on to the village street towards Bradwell quay and the sea, right towards the church, and the American air base, and then out over the marshes towards the ancient Saxon chapel of St Peter's near the sea wall itself. Climb the sea wall and there was the great brown soupy North Sea and always a wild wet wind blowing. I felt always that this place was a part of me, that I belonged here.

My stepfather worked at his writing in his study, wreathed in a fog of tobacco smoke, with a bust of Napoleon and a Confederate flag on his leather-topped desk, whilst my mother tried her very best to tame the house and the garden and us, mostly on her own. We children were never as much help as we should have been, I'm ashamed to say. There were great inglenook fireplaces that devoured logs. So there were always logs for us to fetch in. Then there were the Bramley apples to pick and lay out in the old Nissen huts in the orchard. And if there was nothing that had to be harvested, or dug over or weeded, then there was the jungle of nettles and brambles that had to be beaten back before it overwhelmed us completely. Above all we had not to disturb our stepfather. When he emerged, his work done for the day, we would play cricket on the front lawn, an apple box for a wicket – it was six if you hit it over the wall into the village street. If it rained, we moved into the big vaulted barn where owls and bats and rats and spiders lived, and played fast and furious ping-pong till suppertime.

I slept up in the attic with my elder brother. We had a candle factory up there, melting down the ends of used-up candles on top of a paraffin stove and pouring the wax into jelly moulds. At night we could climb out of our dormer windows and sit and listen to the owls screeching over the marshes, and to the sound of the surging sea beyond. There always seemed to be butterflies in and out of the house – red admirals, peacocks. I collected dead ones in a biscuit tin, laid them out on cotton wool. I kept a wren's nest by my bed, so soft with moss, so beautifully crafted.

My days and nights were filled with the familiarity of the place and its people and of my family. This isn't to say I loved it all. The house was numbingly cold at times. My stepfather could be irritable, rigid and harsh, my mother anxious, tired and sad, my younger siblings intrusive and quarrelsome, and the villagers sometimes very aggressive. What haunted me most though were stories of a house ghost, told for fun, I'm sure, but nonetheless, that ghost terrified me so much that I dreaded going upstairs at night on my own. But all this was home. Haunted or not, this was my place. I belonged.

The day and the moment came always as a shock. So absorbing was this home life of mine, that I'd quite forgotten the existence of my other life. Suddenly I'd find my mother dragging out my school trunk from under the stairs. From that moment on my stomach started to churn. As my trunk filled, I was counting the days, the hours. The process of packing was relentless. Ironing, mending, counting, marking: eight pairs of grey socks, three pairs of blue rugby shorts, two green rugby shirts, two red rugby shirts, green tie, best blazer – red, green and white striped. Evenings were spent watching my mother and my two spinster aunts sewing on nametapes. Every one they sewed on seemed to be cementing the inevitability of my impending expulsion from home. The nametapes read: M.A.B. Morpurgo.

Soon, very soon now, I would be Morpurgo again. Once everything was checked and stitched and darned, the checklist finally ticked off and the trunk ready to go, we drove it to the station to be sent on ahead – luggage in advance, they called it. Where that trunk was going I would surely follow. The next time I'd see it would be only a few days away now, and I'd be back at school. I'd be Morpurgo again.

Those last days hurried by so fast. A last cycle ride to St Peter's, a last walk along the sea wall, the endless goodbyes in the village. 'Cheer up, Michael, you'll be home soon.' A last supper, shepherd's pie, my favourite. But by this time the condemned boy was not eating at all heartily. A last night of fitful sleep, dreading to wake and face the day ahead. I could not look up at my aunts when I said goodbye for fear they would notice the tears and tell me I was 'a big boy and should have grown out of all this by now'. I braved their whiskery embraces and suddenly my mother and I were driving out of the gates, the last chimneys of home disappearing from me behind the trees.

We drove to the station at Southminster. Then we

were in London and on the way to Victoria Station on the Underground. She held my hand now, as we sat silently side by side. We'd done this so many times before. She knew better than to talk to me. My mouth was dry and I felt sick to my stomach. My school uniform, fresh on that morning, was itchy everywhere and constricting. My stepfather had tightened my tie too tight before he said his stiff goodbye, and pulled my cap down so hard that it made my ears stick out even more than they usually did.

Going up the escalator into the bustling smoky concourse of Victoria Station was as I imagined it might be going up the steps on to the scaffold to face my executioner. I never wanted to reach the top because I knew only too well what would be waiting for me. And sure enough, there it was, the first green, white and red cap, the first familiar face. It was Sim, Simpson, my best friend, but I still didn't want to see him. 'Hello Pongo,' he said cheerily. And then to his mother as they walked away: 'That's Morpurgo. I told you about him, remember Mum? He's in my form.'

'There,' my mother said, in a last desperate effort to console me. 'That's your friend. That's Sim, isn't it? It's not so bad, is it?'

What she couldn't know was that it was just about as bad as it could be. Sim was like the others, full of the same hearty cheeriness that would, I know, soon reduce me to tears in the railway carriage.

The caps and the faces multiplied as we neared the platform. There was the master, ticking the names off his list, Mr Stevens (Maths, Geography and Woodwork) who rarely smiled at all at school, but did so now as he greeted me. I knew even then that the smile was not for me, but rather for the benefit of my mother. 'Good to see you back, Morpurgo. He's grown, Mrs Morpurgo. What've you been feeding him?' And they laughed together over my head. The train stood waiting, breathing, hissing, longing – it seemed – to be gone, longing to take me away.

My mother did not wait, as other mothers did, to wave me off. She knew that to do so would simply be prolonging my agony. Maybe it prolonged hers too. She kissed me all too briefly, and left me with her face powder on my cheek and the lingering smell of her. I watched her walk away until I could not see her anymore through my tears. I hoped she would turn around and wave one last time, but she didn't. I had a sudden surging impulse to go after her and cling to her and beg her to take me home. But I hadn't the courage to do it.

'Still the dreamer, Morpurgo, I see,' said Mr Stevens. 'You'd better get on, or the train'll go without you.'

Hauling my suitcase after me I walked along the corridor searching for a window seat that was still empty. Above everything now I needed a window seat so that I could turn away, so they couldn't see my face. Luckily I found something even better, a completely empty carriage. I had it all to myself for just a few precious moments before they came. They came all at once, in a pack, piling in on top of one another, 'bagging' seats, throwing suitcases, full of boisterous jollity. Simpson was there, and Gibbins, Murphy, Sanchez, Webster, Swan, Colman. I did my best to smile at them, but had to look away quickly. They weren't fooled. They'd spotted it. 'Aren't you pleased to see us, Morpurgo?' 'Don't blub, Pongo.' 'It's only school.' 'He wants his mummy wummy.' Then Simpson said, 'Leave him alone.' One thing I had learned was never to rise to the bait. They would stop in time, when they tired of it. And so they did.

As the train pulled out of the station, chuffing and clanking, the talk was all of what they'd done in the 'hols', where they'd been, what new Hornby train set someone had been given on his birthday. By East Croydon, it was all the old jokes: 'Why did the submarine blush?' 'Because it saw Queen Mary's bottom!' 'Why did the chicken cross the road?' 'For some *fowl* reason!' And the carriage rocked with raucous laughter. I looked hard out of my rain-streaked window at the grey green of the Sussex countryside, and cried, silently so that no one would know. But soon enough they did know. 'God, Morpurgo, you go on like that and you'll flood the carriage.' All pretence now abandoned I ran to the toilet where I could grieve privately and loudly.

At East Grinstead station there was the green Southdown coach waiting to take us to school, barely half an hour away. It went by in a minute. Suddenly we were turning in through the great iron gateway and down the gravel drive towards the school. And there it was, looming out of the trees, the dark and forbidding Victorian mansion that would be my prison for fourteen long weeks. With the light on in the front porch it looked as if the school was some great dark monster with a gaping orange mouth that would swallow me up for ever. The Headmaster and his wife were there to greet us, both smiling like crocodiles.

Up in my dormitory I found my bed, my name written on it on sticking plaster – Morpurgo. I was back. I sat down feeling its sagging squeakiness for the first time. That was the moment the idea first came into my head, that I should run away. I began unpacking my suitcase contemplating all the while the dreadful prospect of fourteen weeks away from home. It seemed like I had a life sentence stretching ahead of me with no prospect of remission. Downstairs, outside the Dining Hall, as we lined up for supper and for the prefects' hand inspection I felt suddenly overcome by the claustrophobic smell of the place – floor polish and boiled cabbage. Even then I was still only thinking of running away. I had no real intention of doing it, not yet.

It was the rice pudding that made me do it. Major Philips (Latin and Rugby) sitting at the end of my table told me I had to finish the slimy rice pudding skin I'd hidden under my spoon. To swallow while I was crying was almost impossible, but somehow I managed it, only to retch it up almost at once. Major Philips told me not to be 'childish'. I swallowed again and this time kept it down. This was the moment I made up my mind that I'd had enough, that I was going to run away, that nothing and no one would stop me.

'Please sir,' I asked. 'Can I go to the toilet, successful?' (Successful, in this context, was school code for number twos. If you declared it before you went, you were allowed longer in the toilet and so were not expected back as soon.) But I didn't go to the toilet, successful or otherwise. Once out of the Dining

Hall, I ran for it. Down the brown painted corridor between the framed team photos on both walls, past the banter and clatter and clanging of the kitchens, and out of the back door into the courtyard. It was raining hard under a darkening sky as I sprinted down the gravel drive and out through the great iron gates. I had done it! I was free!

I was thinking out my escape plan as I was running, and trying to control my sobbing at the same time. I would run the two or three miles to Forest Row, hitch a lift or catch a bus to East Grinstead, and then catch the train home. I still had my term's pocket money with me, a ten-shilling note. I could be home in a few hours. I'd just walk in and tell everyone I was never ever going back to that school, that I would never be Morpurgo ever again.

I had gone a mile or so, still running, still sobbing, when a car came by. I had been so busy planning in my head that I hadn't heard the car until it was almost alongside me. My first instinct was to dash off into the fields, for I was sure some master must have seen me escaping and had come after me. I knew full well what would happen if I was caught. It would mean a visit to the Headmaster's study and a caning, six strokes at least; but worse still it would mean capture, back to prison, to rice pudding skin and cabbage, and squeaky beds and Maths and cross-country runs. One glance at the car though told me this was not a master in hot pursuit after all, but a silver-haired old lady in a little black car. She slowed down in front of me and stopped. So I did too. She wound down her window.

'Are you all right, dear?'

'No,' I sobbed.

'You're soaking wet! You'll catch your death!' And then: 'You're from that school up the road, aren't you? You're running away, aren't you?'

'Yes.'

'Where to?'

'Home.'

'Where's home, dear?'

'Essex. By the sea.'

'But that's a hundred miles away. Why don't you

get in the car, dear? I'll take you home with me. Would you like a sticky bun and some nice hot tea?' And she opened the door for me. There was something about her I trusted at once, the gentleness of her smile perhaps, the softness of her voice. That was why I got in, I think. Or maybe it was for the sticky bun. The truth was that I'd suddenly lost heart, suddenly had enough of my great escape. I was cold and wet, and home seemed as far away as the moon, and just as inaccessible.

The car was warm inside, and smelled of leather and dog.

'It's not far dear. Half a mile, that's all. Just in the village. Oh, and this is Jack. He's perfectly friendly.' And by way of introducing himself, the dog in the back began to snuffle the back of my neck. He was a spaniel with long dangly ears and sad bloodshot eyes. And he dribbled a lot.

All the way back to the village, the old lady talked on, about Jack mostly. Jack was ten, in dog years, she told me. If you multiplied by seven, exactly the same age as she was. 'One of the windscreen wipers,' she said, 'only works when it feels like it, and it never feels like it when it's raining.'

I sat and listened and had my neck washed from ear to ear by Jack. It tickled and made me smile. 'That's better, dear,' she said. 'Happier now?'

She gave me more than she'd promised – a whole plate of sticky buns and several cups of tea. She put my soaking wet shoes in the oven to dry and hung my blazer on the clotheshorse by the stove, and she talked all the time, telling me all about herself, how she lived alone these days, how she missed company. Her husband had been killed on the Somme in 1916, in the First World War. 'Jimmy was a Grenadier Guardsman,' she said proudly. 'Six foot three in his socks.' She showed me his photo on the mantelpiece. He had a moustache and lots of medals. 'Loved his fishing,' she went on. 'Loved the sea. We went to the sea whenever we could. Brighton. Lovely place.' On and on she rambled, talking me through her life with Jimmy, and how she'd stayed on in the village after he'd been killed because it was the place they'd known together, how she'd taught in the village school for years before she retired. When the sticky buns were all finished and my shoes were out of the oven and dry at last, she sat back, clapped her hands on her knees, and said:

'Now, dear, what *are* we going to do with you?'

'I don't know,' I replied.

'Shall I telephone your father and mother?'

'No!' I cried. The thought appalled me. They'd be so disappointed in me, so ashamed to know that I'd tried to run away.

'Well then, shall I ring the Headmaster?'

'No! Please don't.' That would be worse still. I'd be up the red-carpeted stairs into his study. I'd been there before all too often. I'd bent over the leather armchair and watched him pull out the cane from behind his desk. I'd waited for the swish and whack, felt the hot searing pain, the stinging eyes, and counted to six. I'd stood up, trembling, to shake his hand and murmured, 'Thank you, sir,' through my weeping mouth. No, not that. Please, not that.

'Maybe,' said the old lady. 'Maybe there's a way round this. You can't have been gone long, an hour or so at most. What if I take you back and drop you off at the top of the school drive? It's nearly dark now. No one would see you, not if you were careful. And with a bit of luck no one would have missed you just yet. You could sneak in and no one would ever know you've run away at all. What d'you think?' I could have hugged her.

Jack came in the car with us in the back seat, licking my neck and my ears all the way. The old lady was unusually silent for a while. Then she said: 'There's something Jimmy once told me not long before he was killed, when he was home on leave for the last time. He never talked much about the war and the trenches, but he did tell me once how scared he was all the time, how scared they all were. So I asked him what made him go on, why he didn't just run away. And he said: "Because of my pals. We're in this together. We look after each other." You've got pals, haven't you, dear?'

'Yes,' I replied, 'but they *like* coming back to school. They *love* it.'

'I wonder if they really do,' she said. 'Maybe they just pretend better than you.'

I was still thinking about that when the car came to a stop. 'I won't go any nearer than this, dear. It wouldn't do for anyone to see you getting out, would it now? Off you go then. And chin up, like my Jimmy.' Jack gave me a goodbye lick as I turned to him, on my nose.

'Thanks for the sticky buns,' I said. She smiled at me and I got out. I watched her drive away into the gloom and vanish. To this day I have no idea who she was. I never saw her again.

I ran down through the rhododendrons and out into the deserted courtyard at the back of the school. The lights were on all over the building, and the place was alive with the sound of children. I knew I needed time to compose myself before I met anyone, so I opened the chapel door and slipped into its enveloping darkness. There I sat and prayed, prayed that I hadn't been found out, that I wouldn't have to face the red-carpeted stairs and the Headmaster's study and the leather chair. I hadn't been in there for more than a few minutes when the door opened and the lights went on.

'Ah, there you are Morpurgo.' It was Mr Morgan (French and Music, and the choirmaster, too). 'We've been looking all over for you.' As he came up the aisle towards me, I knew my prayers had been answered. Mr Morgan was much liked by all of us, because he was invariably kind, and always thought the best of us – rare in that school.

'Bit homesick, are you, Morpurgo?'

'Yes, sir.'

'It'll pass. You'll see.' He put his hand on my shoulder. 'You'd better get yourself upstairs with the others. If you don't get your trunk unpacked by lights out, Matron will eat you alive, and we don't want that, do we?'

'No, sir.'

And so I left Mr Morgan and the chapel and went upstairs to my dormitory. 'Where've you been? I thought you'd scarpered, run away,' said Simpson, unpacking his trunk on the bed next to mine.

'I just felt a bit sick,' I said. Then I opened my trunk.

On the top of my clothes was a note and three bars of Cadbury's chocolate. The note read: 'Have a good term. Love Mum.' Simpson spotted the chocolate, and pounced. Suddenly everyone in the dormitory was around me, and at my chocolate, like gannets. I managed to keep a little back for myself, which I hid under my pillow, and ate late that night as I listened to the bell in the clock tower chiming midnight. As it finished I heard Simpson crying to himself, as silently as he could.

'You all right, Sim?' I whispered.

'Fine,' he sniffed. And then, 'Pongo, did you scarper?'

'Yes,' I said.

'Next time you go, take me with you. Promise?'

'Promise,' I replied.

But I never did scarper again. Perhaps I never again plucked up the courage; perhaps I listened to the old lady's advice. I've certainly never forgotten it. It was my one and only great escape.

Paul Jennings

Strap Stopper

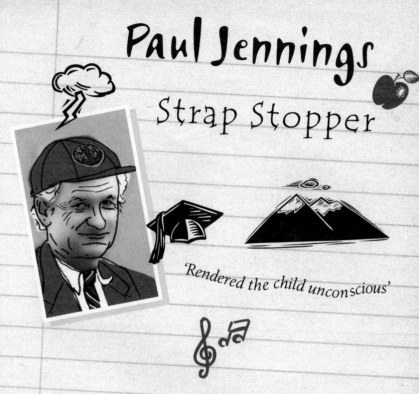

'Rendered the child unconscious'

PAUL JENNINGS was born in England but went to live in Australia when he was six. He became a teacher and then a lecturer, first in Special Education and then in Language and Literature. His first book Unreal! was published in 1987 which won the Young Australians' Best Book Award which he then went on to win eleven times with other titles! In the Australia Day 1995 Honours List he was appointed Member in the General Division of the Order of Australia for services to children's literature. His television series Round the Twist won the Prix Jeunesse Award and in 2001 he won a COOL Award for The Paw Thing which was declared the 'Coolest Book of the Decade'.

Paul Jennings

Strap Stopper

These days kids don't get the strap in schools. And a good thing too.

I don't think I was a particularly bad boy at school but I did seem to get the strap a lot. We called it, 'getting the cuts.' The thought of it hung over my head like a rain cloud. Every school day this cloud followed me around. At any moment it might turn into a storm which would engulf me totally.

That was the awful thing. Not knowing when the cloud was going to break. Not knowing when I might do something which would incur the wrath of the particularly awful teacher I had that year. His name was Mr Down but we always called him Downie.

I remember him walking into the classroom on the first day of school. What was he going to be like? A wonderful human being who would fill your year with fun and laughter? A tyrant who would leave you trembling all day? A weakling who would let his pupils run all over him? No one knew. The class fell silent. Every eye watched his slightest move.

He walked over to the side of the wooden cupboard at the front of the room. He opened the door and took out a hammer and a nail. He banged the nail loudly into the side of the cupboard. Each thump echoed around the room and made us shake. Finally he unrolled a long leather strap from his pocket and hung it on the nail.

We all quivered. We knew the answers to our questions and he hadn't even spoken a word.

This man made fifty-two children's lives miserable for a year. One minute you would be innocently sitting there minding your own business and the next you were hauled out in front of the class and publicly punished.

I could live with getting the strap for doing something genuinely bad. But not for nothing. It hurt much more to be strapped when you were innocent.

Once when I was puzzling over a page of sums I

remember chewing the end of a red pencil and pressing it thoughtfully against my forehead.

'Jennings,' roared a loud voice. 'You've got the measles.' I looked up in astonishment. I felt quite well but I hoped it was true. A week off school with the measles was a week less suffering in the classroom. Downie bent over and inspected my head more closely. The red spots were not spots at all. They were dots made by the end of my wet pencil.

Little veins bulged out on Downie's face. He dragged me out the front and gave me six of the best.

I remember walking home nursing my sore hand and saying to myself, 'When I grow up I am going to find Downie and flatten him. I will bash him up. I will pay him back one day.'

I nursed my hatred for this man every day. On the way to school I would sing a little song to myself that I had made up based on an old rhyme.

Bald head Down
Went to town

Riding on a pony
Stuck a feather up his bum
And called it macaroni

It's funny – I was never one to use bad language, but this act of secret defiance made me feel a little better in my silent suffering.

Don't get me wrong. Sometimes, like everyone else I did stupid things. Once, at break-time I found a large apple in my lunchbag. For some unknown reason I decided to throw it into the air high above the playground. At the very moment the apple left my hand I saw Downie watching me. With our eyes we both traced the high arc of the apple's journey into the sky. For a moment it almost seemed to be going into orbit. But then it froze and fell towards earth. A girl named Julia was innocently skipping and laughing in the playground.

Julia was Downie's favourite. He always chose her to arrange the flowers or clean the blackboard.

Oh the fear. The terror. In a fraction of a second the

whole picture froze into my brain. I knew. I just knew what was going to occur.

Smash. The apple hit Julia fair on the head. The apple splattered into a million fragments and she dropped to the ground like a stone.

Mrs Henderson who taught the infants rushed over. 'What happened?' she yelled at Downie.

He grabbed me by the ear and spat out, 'This, this…' He couldn't find a bad enough word to describe me. 'Threw an apple at the girl and rendered the child unconscious.'

Julia was taken to the sick-room where she rapidly recovered.

Downie dragged me off and strapped me six times. I never recovered.

His words, *'Rendered the child unconscious,'* burned into my brain. I felt terribly guilty. I had hurt Julia. It was thoughtless. What a fool I was.

Sometimes I would lie in bed and say the words to myself. 'Rendered the child unconscious.' I would roll them around in my mouth like some unpleasant medicine that I just couldn't bring myself to swallow. After that, Downie would find any excuse to give me the strap. He had a million ways of making me suffer.

It was always worse if you had to wait for several hours or days before your punishment was administered. I recall one particular incident really well.

'Three boys were seen playing in the clay hills,' said Downie one day.

We all looked at each other. All the kids played in the clay hills after school even though you weren't supposed to. Three people were going to be strapped. Everyone froze. Well, all the boys did anyway.

Girls were never given the strap so they didn't have to worry. But the boys were constantly talking about it. There were many theories about ways to stop it hurting. If you pulled your hand away you got an extra whack for your trouble. And if the teacher hit his own leg you might infuriate him. I never pulled my hand away.

I did try curling up my palm a couple of times but

Downie would always flatted out my fingers with a mocking grin. Most kids agreed that it was definitely not worth letting Mr Down have an excuse to give you more.

'Jennings, Simons and Humphries,' said Downie. 'Report to me after school.' The three of us gasped in horror. Oh no. It was me. I was in it.

At lunchtime, the boys who were not going to be strapped gathered around. They were full of unhelpful advice.

'Go first and get it over with,' said Jeffries.

I looked at him balefully. It was all very well to say, 'Go first.' But when the time came you would do anything to put the pain off for a few more seconds. No one ever wanted to be first.

'Rub this stuff into your hand,' said my friend Foxy, 'and it won't hurt when you get the cuts.' He handed me a lump of waxy, yellow substance.

'What is it?'

'Rosin,' said Foxy. 'Rosin Strap Stopper. My cousin gave it to me. He swears that it stops the pain. You won't feel a thing I promise you. It won't hurt a bit.'

I took the rosin hopefully. It was better than nothing. The rosin was passed from hand to hand and we rubbed it into our fingers and palms at every chance we got. I found a small stick and gave myself a gentle tap.

'It still hurts,' I said.

'It only works on really hard whacks,' said Foxy. 'It's guaranteed to work on the strap.'

The day wore on slowly. Oh the terror. There was just a chance, a small chance, that we would get a lecture and nothing worse. All day, like condemned men in their cells, we waited. But in our hearts we knew it was going to be the strap. Thank goodness for the Strap Stopper.

Finally the dreaded moment came. The three of us stood shaking on the platform at the front of the empty classroom. Simons' face was clammy and pale. Humphries stood defiantly, not showing his fear. I felt sick.

'Line up,' said Downie as he took the strap down from its nail.

No one moved.

'You first Simons.'

Beads of sweat started to trickle down Simons' temples. With trembling knees he moved forward.

'Then you, Humphries.'

Humphries moved into second place. I was last in line.

Poor Simons. I had never seen anyone look so scared. His face was white.

'Hold out your hand.'

Simons held out his hand. The poor kid. He was absolutely filled with terror. 'Whack,' down came the leather strap. Simons' face froze. Then he just dropped to the floor like a sack of wheat.

Now it was Downie who turned pale. He bent down and shook Simons' head. No response. Simons had fainted.

Then I noticed something I had never seen before. Downie was worried. He glared at me.

'Quick,' he said. 'Fetch Mrs Henderson.'

I turned to go but Downie grabbed my shoulder

and thrust the strap towards my face.

'Not a word about *this*,' he said. He shoved the strap into a drawer and closed it.

I rushed out of the room and returned with Mrs Henderson.

'What happened?' she said.

No one answered. Even Downie seemed lost for words.

I couldn't think what to say. There were four months of school left. If I told about the strap I would be history. And anyway, we were only kids. What could we do?

I tried to search for words. Nothing would come. I tried to force out a few words. Suddenly my mouth seemed to go into automatic drive. I just couldn't stop it.

'He rendered the child unconscious,' I said.

Mrs Henderson didn't seem to understand.

'What's this yellow stuff on his hands?' she said urgently as she bent over Simons' slumped figure.

'Strap Stopper,' said Humphries. He nervously

blurted out the whole story. Mrs Henderson threw a quick glance at Downie and then helped him carry Simons out to her car. She told Humphries and I to follow. She took us to the local doctor and our parents were called. The doctor was very kind.

To us.

He didn't seem to like Downie at all.

'This yellow stuff could be poisonous,' he said. 'It could have seeped through their skin. These boys had better stay home in bed until I find out what's in it.'

We were given a whole week off school. Wonderful, wonderful, wonderful.

Poor old Simons couldn't remember a thing. And Humphries and I had escaped. So there hadn't been any pain at all. The Strap Stopper turned out not to be poisonous but it had saved the day.

When we went back to school Downie had gone. Moved to another school. I only saw him once more, many years later.

My next teacher was Mr Hooper. A wonderful man who filled our life with joy and laughter. He showed slides of his travels around Australia and amazed us with his stories of mountain climbing and exploring Antarctica. He loved music and had the whole class singing at every opportunity. There was no fear. No strap. I loved school. I couldn't wait to get there. The days and weeks just flew by.

My only regret was not telling him how much I had appreciated being in his class. I was too shy and at the end of the school year I just gave him a small present like everyone else. He never knew what joy he had given to all of us.

When I moved on to secondary school, I found that they didn't use the strap at all. They had the cane instead. It was a long, thin stick that stung like the blazes. I only received it once.

I was never any good at football and it was my practice to sneak off and read in the library instead. The librarian knew what I was up to but she kept quiet about it. I was safely hidden because other classes would be in there doing research and no one noticed an extra student.

One day, however, the library was empty. The Headmaster came in and found only one boy reading quietly in a corner.

'Why aren't you at sport, Jennings?'

'I like reading better, sir,' I said in a weak voice. 'And I hate footy.'

He took me off to his office and gave me three stinging whacks on the hand.

Many years later when I was a man I received a letter from that school. It was from the librarian. She told me that the boys loved my books and would I come and speak to them about writing stories.

I went and I have to say that I enjoyed talking to those students and looking around the library that had been my refuge so long ago.

I told the boys a lot of stories that I had made up and put into books. But I didn't tell them the true yarn about getting the cane. Sometimes it is better to keep quiet.

Later I grew up to be a teacher myself. On one particular day when I was visiting the Education

Department I found myself in a lift with a small, bald man. It was Downie. I towered over him. He seemed weak and old and unhappy.

My childhood thoughts of bashing him up came flooding into my head. As the lift headed upwards I stood there next to him chewing the familiar words silently like bad medicine.

'He rendered the child unconscious.'

The lift doors opened and Downie walked out. My angry thoughts vanished with him and the doors closed on that part of my life forever. Well almost.

Ten years later I applied for a job as a lecturer at a teachers' college. On my first day in the new position I read down the list of staff members named in the college handbook. I noticed the name, Mr Hooper, the marvellous teacher who had told us tales about exploring in Antarctica.

I rushed around to his office and thanked him for the wonderful year he gave me at school. 'I have never forgotten you,' I told him. 'It was the happiest year of my life.'

We both stared at each other with tears in our eyes. I could tell that he was very moved.

When I got home I rummaged around in the drawers of my desk. Finally I found what I was looking for. I took out the lump of yellow rosin. And dropped it into the bin.

It didn't hurt a bit.

Michael Rosen

'Tilly-vally, Lady!'

Twelfth Night

MICHAEL ROSEN is a poet, author and radio and television presenter. He has won awards for all aspects of his work including a Talkies award for the best poetry tape of the year, Parent Magazine Award for the best picture book of the year, a Glenfiddick Award for the best radio programme of the year and the Eleanor Farjeon Award for his contribution to children's literature. We're Going on A Bear Hunt won the Smarties Award and Quick, Let's Get out of Here won the Signal Poetry Award. His poetry collections include Mind Your Own Business, You Can't Catch Me, Wouldn't You Like to Know, Centrally Heated Knickers, Lunch Boxes Don't Fly and Uncle Billy Being Silly.

Michael Rosen

'Tilly-vally, Lady!'

If there was one thing I wanted to be, above everything else, it was to be an actor. No, that wasn't strictly true. If I could learn to play the harmonica a bit better, I could be like John Lennon in the Beatles or Mick Jagger in the Rolling Stones. No, no, no, what I really wanted to do was play for England. No – actually that wasn't true either. If there was one thing I wanted to be, it was to be a politician. Yes, that was it. To be a politician and save the world from poverty and nuclear bombs. Oh no, wait a minute. There was something else. If there was one thing I wanted to be, it was to be a writer.

I was thinking all this instead of learning my lines for the play I was in. It was *Twelfth Night* by William Shakespeare. And I was Sir Toby Belch. It was three nights to go to the opening night and I hadn't learned my lines. The director was getting twitchy; Mr James. Mr Dickie James, the chemistry teacher. Short and plump, he smoked a pipe and he was a diabetic. This meant that sometimes he would doze off in front of us. If this happened we were under instruction from him to rush up and immediately give him something to eat, ideally a sugar lump or a bit of chocolate. He told us that he had a sugar lump in his jacket pocket. We just had to dive into this pocket, find the sugar lump and get it into his mouth.

But now, he was enjoying himself, directing the play. He strutted about waving his arms in the air. I had to bawl out, 'Tilly-vally, Lady!' I'm not sure even now what it means. Something like 'stuff and nonsense', perhaps. Sir Toby Belch is old, drunk, fat and mischievous. He's also a sponger – someone who lives off other people's money and kindness. 'Tilly-vally, Lady!' shouts Mr James, waving his arm in the air. 'Say it to the whole world, Michael. It's a big hall. They all want to hear it. Do you know the words to this scene?'

I didn't.

Mr James is getting seriously twitchy. 'Let's do the catch,' he says.

A 'catch' is what these days we would call a 'round', like *London's Burning*. I had to sing the catch with two other people. They could both sing. I couldn't. I'm OK when I'm singing along with others, but in a catch, like a round, you have to sing *against* the others. While they're singing one thing, I have to sing something else. I was having trouble getting it right. I had to sing, 'Hold thy peace, I prithee hold thy peace, thou knave... COUNT TWO ...Hold thy peace thou knave... COUNT FOUR... Thou knave.'

'You get it, don't you?' said Dickie.

'What?'

'"Hold thy peace",' he said. 'Look, I *think* we can get away with this. "Piece", in Shakespeare's time meant your thing. You know, what do you call it?'

'Dickie?'

'Alright, alright. Well, you could look like you're holding your piece, while you're singing it, couldn't you? OK, try it, and try and enjoy the damn thing, will you?

You're all supposed to be drunk, and we're all supposed to think it's hilariously funny. If you can't count the beats to yourself, you can count them out loud if you like.'

'Hold thy peace, I prithee hold thy peace, one two...'

'Good!' roared Mr James from the back of the hall. 'You're getting it. OK, now get yourselves off home. Learn those lines, Michael, and we go for a first dress rehearsal tomorrow night.'

Fair enough, except *this* night, there was something else on. The school rugby team had challenged the local girls' school's netball team to a game of basketball in the gym. Tonight. In fancy dress. Even now, they would be getting ready.

I slipped out the back and over to the gym. And it was already underway. I had in my bag parts of a Dracula outfit: including a top hat that lies flat. When you bash it against your chest it pops up into a proper hat. I stepped out into the middle of the match, banged the hat and put it on. Applause.

I was useless at basketball and that was the point. I was the useless one. They passed me the ball and I would give it to the girls. Again and again. Laughter. Applause. Then it was time for home. Out into the night. Only a week to go until Christmas. At home, the house was decorated. But now, the same old nightly problem of getting there.

The walk to the train station, the last on the line. You could see it across the field at the back of the school. The lights from the platform made a globe in the dark, and then the luminous caterpillar of a train would crawl in and wait. If it was already there, I'd have to run for it, hoping that it wouldn't pull out before I arrived panting on to the platform. If I missed it, there would be half an hour to wait for another. At this time of night, I'd be on my own. Then it was four stops down the line. Out, wait for a bus, and then the final walk home, along an unlit road to where our house stood, alone at the top of a hill, overlooking fields and woods.

Not that this was the country. This was the suburbs. The kind of place that's full of long lonely streets where nothing happens. On the edge of the big city where everything happens and where I'd really like to be.

I ran towards the white globe of the station. The train was waiting. I could hear the mini-mini-mini-mini-mini of its electric engines turning over. Down the steps and into the train, the doors closed with a sigh and thud. My brother could do all these noises. He was away at university now, but he'd be back soon for Christmas. We'd have a good one this year, I was sure. People would come and see *Twelfth Night* and if I was good enough maybe my parents would say that, yes, one day I could be an actor. They wanted me to be a doctor. Funny that, being a doctor wasn't on my list of great things I wanted to be.

On the train, I peered out into the night. I could just make out the canal as it picked up the lights of my train. Away in the distance, cars flicked along the new road, dashing from one pool of light to the next. I was glad they had liked the top hat trick. It was a real nineteenth-century hat that posh gents took to the opera. It seems as if they could sit on them while the opera was on, and then when it was time to go, they stood up, popped them out and put them on. The end of an opera, after the applause, used to be full of the sound of hats popping.

In my rucksack was homework, homework, homework. Big exams were coming up and all the work I had done, should have done, might have done, wouldn't do, was all sitting in a big spring-back file. My old grey rucksack, the one that smelled of camping holidays.

The train rambled on to my stop and I climbed out and up the steps to the bus stop. Why did my parents move here? Why did we move further away from the city, out to this place that was nowhere? Yes, I know we were 'evicted'. That word. The landlord threw us out of the flat over a shop where I had always lived. Even so, I didn't know what we were doing stuck out in this place overlooking nothing, next to nothing.

When I got home, I would sit down and work on my lines. 'Tilly-vally, Lady!' And that burp thing. I had to burp and then shout, 'A plague upon this pickled herring'. The herring was supposed to have made me burp. And wasn't it amazing – I loved pickled herring! Apart from my parents and grandparents, I was the only person in the world I knew who liked pickled herring. I loved hoisting the slimy grey herring out of the jar and chewing it up with the bits of raw onion. Sometimes a whole pepper corn would hide amongst the onion and it would explode in my mouth.

The bus ground up the hill to the hospital. The world famous hospital where men from the RAF who had been burned-up in their planes had had their faces re-made. I spent a week here when my nose was broken. In the ward there was a guy with scarcely a face on him. He showed me a photo of himself before his car accident. He had looked like Elvis. And just across the road, opposite the hospital itself, hadn't our friend Andy been killed?

Ride on round the bend, past the arch which you could see in the background of that famous film about a veteran car race from London to Brighton. That's where I had to get off, because the bus turned off there and I had to walk the rest of the way home.

No pavement here, just heathland. A pub, with coloured lights in the tree outside and then nothing. Just the road, and the night, and me walking towards the light of our kitchen at the top of the hill. Once, just as I was walking past the pub, two men jumped out from behind the tree and grabbed my bag. I screamed and they explained they were policemen.

But now I was on my own. Should I walk on the path? No, the branches from the hawthorn bushes, full of prickles, were overhanging too low and I didn't fancy walking along bending down, ducking under the thorns. Especially as I was so tired. No, I would walk in the road. It was only a few hundred yards and there was our kitchen light up ahead. I'd make myself a big fat sandwich. Maybe there'd be some pickled herring and I could practice the burp.

I woke up in a hospital ward. By the side of my bed was someone in a wheelchair. In the beds all around me were young blokes with their legs hanging from the bar over their beds. Motorbike accidents. And I was hanging from the bar too. Lying in a kind of sling round my middle that was swinging from the bar.

My mother was there, drumming my arm with her finger. And soon more people were there too: everyone who had been at the basketball game, and everyone in *Twelfth Night* and everyone who used the same train home and everyone who knew me from the old school and all the people who worked with my dad and all the people who worked with my mum and all the cousins and the uncles and the aunts and... Mr James.

They told me that I had been hit in the back by a car. The driver had driven on until he got to the police station. There he had told them he had hit someone. They drove back to the spot and I wasn't there. The police told my father that they thought the man was drunk. Perhaps he had just imagined it. They were just about to go when they heard a noise from down the bank by the side of the road. Someone talking. They said it was something to do with picked herring and something else about a lady called Tilly or a valley. They went to look and I was lying there talking. With not a scratch on me. I talked to them, told them who I was, where I had been, where I was going. My parents had spent the night with me, waiting for the X-ray, the X-ray that showed I had broken my pelvis. The bit at the front had come apart. Just like when a woman has a baby, they said. And now I was in a sling, hanging from a bar, to help it come together and I didn't remember a single bit of the story. Last thing I remembered was deciding to walk in the road instead of under the thorn bushes.

'It seems like your rucksack saved you,' my father said. He showed me the spring-back file full of the work I had done and should do. It was smashed in.

Mr James asked the nurse if she thought I'd be well enough to do the play. 'What?' she said. '*Well* enough?' She was very small and Danish. '*Well* enough?! He's going to be in that sling for ten weeks.'

Poor Mr James. He looked down at the ground. It had all gone wrong.

'So who's going to do it?' I asked.

'I'll have to,' he said.

'Do you know the words?' I said.

'As well as you do,' he said.

And so Mr James played Sir Toby Belch, the family had Christmas in the house on the hill, the Beatles brought out their *All My Loving* album and the whole world went mad for them. And I lay in bed thinking: if there was one thing I wanted to be above everything else it was to be an actor. No, that wasn't strictly true. If I could learn to play the harmonica a bit better, I could be like John Lennon in the Beatles or Mick Jagger in the Rolling Stones. No, no, no what I really I wanted to do was play for England. No – actually that wasn't true either. If there was one thing I wanted to be it was to be a politician. Yes, that was it. To be a politician and save the world from poverty and nuclear bombs. Oh no, wait a minute. There was something else. If there was one thing I wanted to be it was to be a writer.